LIMBERLOST III

The Prequel

by

RICKY DALE

Limberlost III

Spiderwize
Remus House
Coltsfoot Drive
Woodston
Peterborough
PE2 9BF

www.spiderwize.com

A CIP catalogue record for this book is available from the British Library.

Photo restoration by Paul & Gail Freathy

LIMBERLOST III

THE PREQUEL

**"WHO. AFTER ALL. KNOWS WHO WE REALLY ARE OR WHERE WE ARE
GOING?**

WE ARE ALL, IN A WAY, CARRIED ONWARDS BY A GREYHOUND BUS" ...

AUTHOR'S NOTE

When I began to write Limberlost (book I) back in 2006, it was initially as a stopgap measure whilst my daughter was attending college/ university. I assumed that the finalized novel might make an interesting read for family and friends – and conceivably a mixed assortment of booksellers/readers.

However, Limberlost (book I) was essentially going to be a 'one off'. Its intention was to chronicle the bold, elegant and heartbreakingly charismatic presence of someone who floated by in a period of my early life. Viz: Krystyna (a.k.a. Kim).

After Limberlost (book I) was published - and for reasons not entirely clear to me at that time -I began receiving messages from across the U.K. and Canada asking (nay questioning!) "whatever happened to Krystyna (Kim)?"

And so with that in mind and for all of you very especial early readers and for anyone else with such curiosity - I am resolved to apprise you all of the entire 'Krystyna' (Kim) epic in sequel and prequel format.

There is no order in which each of the three novels are read - the story of Krystyna and her 'family' is quite abundantly unsystematic, you know! Be that as it may; whatever order you do decide upon, I am confident that you will discover, among other things, many and many more mesmerizing eventualities. I am absolutely sure that they will all encompass your heart and cause you to both weep and cheer - and perhaps abstractedly hear Kim sing once again - I hope, I hope!

Contents

**** Principal characters ****

Kim Denisa - Birth name Krystyna Comanescu. Lyric soprano, whose misshapened heart well-nigh sang along

Sandra - Concert pianist, who is playin' it cool and shakin' down the World

Dahlia Carriera - Showgirl, whose envying beauty is even on the face of strangers

Renek Comanescu - Krystyna's Father, who kept his empty heart alive longer than he should

Bliss Carmen - Maiden name Provenzano. Earliest proprietor of Limberlost and who has always been the 'angel on the bedpost'

Lillian Carmen - AKA 'Mom'. Restaurateur; daughter of Bliss who is an aphrodisiac with an ultraviolet jab!

Joe Burke - Cowboy, who every man would like to be on any given Sunday

LeParrain - Capo dl tutti capi of South-Central Ontario, whose unpardonable crime would be the killing of a kitty cat

Jim Castellano - Organisation Lieutenant, who is the deviser of new solutions to old problems

Redvers Lamar-Smith - Mayor of Anville, who will not be voted in again 'till 'Rocky' runs for Mayor!

Leroy Strooduhs - Theatrical Broker, who always was a disillusioned moth flapping at the window of indiscernibility

Jacques Leyrac - Impresario extraordinaire, who was a friend of James Dean

Bob Mitcham - Michigan Lay Preacher, who prefers to pray at empty shrines

Sarah Smith - Adolescent Iroquoian, whose taste for love too soon went wrong

George Zalokostas - Chicken Farmer, who is cut off from the world by Buffalo grass

Alice - Who is a retired Anville 'teacher of respectable disposition'

Tony Barber - Barber, who is nothardly a hairdresser!

<u>DEDICATED</u>

To my daughter, Dr. Kim Jayne, who in 2001 walked with me along the bank of Winter Creek.

ACKNOWLEDGEMENT

The author wishes to express his gratitude to <u>Zoë Hatherall</u> and to <u>Pete Layland</u> for their kind words and considerate encouragement during the long years it took to write this trilogy.

The last 'round-up'; before the story proper

IS TRUTH STRANGER

THAN FICTION?

Here, contained in the pages of these Limberlost novels is the haunting account of a real 'Family'. It is an extraordinary semi-epic as strong and as varied as any North American fiction can offer.

If indeed you are influenced by the chewiness of words and with lavishly long sentences then watch out, because all of the Limberlost characters are going to rise up from out of these pages to meet you; as scene after scene comes to life. Not only will you see them but you will even capture their voices!

About the time that you have finished reading these sentences, you will find yourself wondering why for heavens sake did it take three books in order to write a compartmentalization about a family?

Don't ask!

Don't talk!

Don't tell!

These books are only meant for all of you with the good sense to remain tight-lipped: their mysteries are too perilous and painful to be aired indiscriminately.
And so in other words it's recommended that you approach 'Limberlost' with a willing suspension of your disbelief. Because with so much thrown together in these novels, they will demand a second or third reading before you can categorically tell whether or not truth is indeed much stranger than fiction!

PREFACE [to the Prequel]

It may be that there comes a point in everyone's life when their indecision versus their decisiveness can result in a significant stumbling block. Having said that, 'sitting on the fence' is nothardly the worse alternative, unless you are not necessarily afraid of what's upcoming - or what has gone before. Nevertheless, I still have a tendency toward an apprehensive reckoning regarding the 'nothing' left to learn versus the 'something' that I inadvertently failed to learn! The only understanding I have gained is that the whole donnybrook has become one of those semi-auspicious deals. And no matter how valuable the darkness is, the occasion feels considerably more affable with all the nightlights burning. Perhaps to some extent I am running slightly scared; stumbling and bumbling in a pathetic attempt to discover a compassionate equilibrium of sorts. The truth is that I've invested far too much of my precious time forgetting to remember precisely what it was I originally set out to forget! The conclusion is really simplistic and both reasonable and responsible: even if I could go back, I wouldn't and even if I could, I couldn't!

Ridiculous though it sounds I feel every bit compelled to scribble a despairing begging message and forward it 'special delivery' to Walt Whitman; it seems to me that only that brave American of all-innocentness would be qualified to provide me with the answer I so desire. Although from time to time I have faced much more difficult dilemmas, absolutely none of them have been quite so emotionally draining. To be metaphorically candid I would much prefer to place my totally confused brain in the feeble hands of some white-haired poet who has grown tired of trying to understand the limited reasoning of others and therefore, would be so inclined to an introspective view point. I imagine that merely to sit at Walt Whitman's desk would be an inroad to modest salvation!

Especially at times like these I feel that I am so many miles and infinite worlds from any semblance that was her or is her., and more and more I wonder if that blinding distance is really my advantage and is as compatible as the closeness once was. In any event I had scarcely imagined that at some unspecified time on some random afternoon, her telephone message would once again fill my head with the incredulous libretto of opening my ink pot once again.   When I finally become wide awake and rearrange my bewildered face in the mirror, I begin to become thoroughly aware that even now she still has the ability to command at least 49 per cent of my total existence; possibly more! In any event, the 'leftovers' are in all likelihood far too jejune to feel concern about!

Periodically, you may see me running along the beach; kicking the sand up from out of the dunes; letting the tide roll over me - or skating across a frozen lake and diving headlong into the drifts of virgin snow: oblivious that winter had even arrived. You may have even heard me singing like a latter day Elvis or barrelling down the freeway like Steve McQueen.   Directly because, that is the part of me that she is the owner of. It is as though she is a miraculous snowflake with an echo that only you can hear; and if you should hesitate to prick-up your ears, your brain would quickly revert back to the embryo it previously was. She was able to perceive no matter what voids there happened to be, sneaking insidiously around in your life. She could see them for the apathetic apple sauce that they are and consequently she would win victories over them with you again and again.

And what of the part of her that you owned? Every song she sang and word she uttered were confined to just you. She respected every significant syllable; it was as though they were of her very own creation and she projected this certainty to you, her listener. She was the only artist or person I had ever seen who could do this; even more than her desire to share her music she was impulsed into wanting above all else to share 'herself'. Her overall homage to every note was multiplied by her search for a platonic love affair with every human soul.

Resolve: some songs do not exist without the singer and even some brilliant poetry can become trapped and forsaken among a multitude of rhymes. Perhaps my role is to unmask the singer, similar to that of a meticulous archaeologist; who, with the greatest of care is able to peel off the non-transparent matter that covers each sentence - in order to make them visually conspicuous. I am concerned, however, that in doing so I could inadvertently be betraying a confidence. Although I am relatively comfortable in my capacity as her biographer - to all intents and purposes a kind of 'go-between' in the physical world, to her intensely unique world - nonetheless, I have no unpardonable wish to become her Judas Iscariot!

I was riding through the city on a train when I eventually began to string a few words together. My source of inspiration was most probably ignited by several youngsters chalking messages upon the train yards. Like a scholar poring over unpublished manuscripts, I was eager to read what they were writing. I suppose in a peculiar way we were both on a mission; but as the train twisted amid a maze of tracks, I was never to realize where their theme ended or indeed where mine was to begin. When I finally put pen back to paper, it was as though all of the symbols to my sentences were in a state of preparedness upon the blank paper - pure supposition of course, but I knew it stretched a lot further than sheer wishfulness.

Resolve rescinded: Some things I can only guess at and never hope to really understand what ongoing significance they may have had. And although she has assured me of her constancy (regardless of repercussions) I alone have decided to go contrary to her wishes. My final drop of ink is spent, the time has come to nail-up all the windows and doors of Limberlost I and II, turn off all the faucets, disconnect the hydro and redirect the mail. It is not a decision that I wish to be involved in - to betray a confidence, whether by consent or otherwise.

Resolve restored... It's late, and I sit a nearly breathless moment on the bed's edge; kick off my slippers, click off the radio and then the light. Across the jet blackness of inevitable doubt I catch sight of her: Lit cigarette between her slim fingers, arms gesticulating; articulating; exhilarating my senses with persuasiveness; a tinge of strawberry hues the blackness and I become aware of my frail complicity. A moment disappears and the light clicks on; as if by another hand other than my own. I get up off the bed, go out through the bedroom door to my desk and commence to write the absolute chapters; like perhaps I really ought to have done at the beginning.

LIMBERLOST III - The Prequel

CHAPTER ONE

Résumé...

... resigning myself to one more ashtray and gazing out upon an immensely balmy afternoon; I sipped pleasantly upon my first taste of iced-tea with lemon slice.

It was September 1959 when I first discovered the fabled Lido Deck of the fabulous Brant Inn; nestling proud upon the shore of the indomitable Lake Ontario.

The Brant and I were on the brink of embarking upon an exclusive and comparatively lengthy relationship; in return for my youth it vowed to award me with far more than I ever could have imagined.

It was as though we were treading identical parallel paths in our own temporized odyssey of destiny; and that the inevitability of tired eyes, acned scars and mechanical devices would eventually and obnoxiously federate and bring about our demise. However, in spite of all the unsympatheticness that would occur, even so I easily managed to capture and keep all the warmth that the Brant had entrusted me with.

Not to imagine the beguiling melodies that had floated out across the lake at sundown is inconceivable, there are not enough anomalous floods of time that could ever sweep such abiding memories away.

Not all of my evergreen contemplations are of a relatively ethereal nature. I recall how bowled over I was after being invited to the undreamed of palatial penthouse of Brant supremo John Murray Anderson.

One very distinct evening, in the blink of an eye we were visited in the penthouse by the lustrous Johnnie Ray. He reminisced about getting fired from Hamilton's Flamingo Tavern some 12 years earlier - that was before his trademark hit 'Cry'.

Most dear to me especially is the irrepressible Danny Kay. One evening we staged a humorous little scene together in the penthouse, specifically intended for Mr Anderson.

From the first time I met her, I confess to having the 'hots' over the genuinely charming Jayne Mansfield. Realistically her comportment was entirely 'sisterly' - mine however, was more inclined to be rather an incestuous alteration of a sister! However, it was generally the terrible taste of the 'Hat Check' girls' kisses that I would compensate myself with at the end of each evening.

As we all talked and laughed into the dawning, there was always something new and exciting to be gained during those droll decades.

Even now, every memorable moment still splendidly survives; as pristine and as unruffled, like the golden sunlit dust they have become. Strange though it may seem now, I was for the most part totally unknowing of the Brant's highly regarded reputation. In this neck of the woods I had very little familiarity with such establishments, and viewed the Brant as rather a staid nightspot for 'older folk'. For me it was a reasonable someplace, somewhere where I was able to wink at the camera, get heard on 900 CHML and respectably earn a buck.

You see, I'd got it all pretty much worked out - I wasn't really particularly that bothered by starry-eyed aspirations of spilling my fallaciously 'fabulous' voice across the province. What was more significant to me is that 'singing' was inclined to be a lot more preferable than digging out troughs last winter in depressing sub-zero Chippewa - since that was my erstwhile alternative!

'Singing' was perhaps predominately my getaway from that sort of indigence, and a contented assurance that I could stretch to another pack of smokes. So there I was; bib, tuckered, polished and meticulously over-rehearsed and waiting in turn to be evaluated again. I was likely as not to be by far the most wet behind the ears teenage entertainer to rub shoulders with the enumerate masters who graced the Brants hallowed portals; however, it was not the way that I perceived matters at that time.

Being raised in 'British' West Africa had both its misconceptions and its consequences. Long before I had reach puberty I'd been majorly inculcated with the colonists' attitude of superiority. And, so, with all my inbuilt 'holier-than-thou' principles I felt really quite philosophical about the forthcoming audition. I easily understood that my 'reflection' was invaluably not less than perfect and therefore, to all intents and purposes the suggestion of rejection was simply absurd.

However, perspectives like horizons do out of the blue change; and as often as not when they do, yesterdays acceptable answers unexpectedly become today's refreshed questions.

It never occurred to me on that nonchalant especial afternoon, that all of us ingenious mortals on hand, were close to finding our unelaborated raison d'etre. And that musically, there would probably never be such an authoritative comparison to the expression. By the same token, it seems to me that I had spent my lifetime searching and moving toward that moment of perfection; and upon reflection, it convinced me to comfy down with myself. Perhaps in the realization that the onward journey to normality would lack such exacting exuberance.

It's true, none of us were entirely prepared for the phenomenon that was Krystyna Comanescu - an inconspicuous, rustic young woman from Aurora Ontario.

The question was, and still is - does Aurora boast operatic tutoring of such calibre? And in any event why nominate the Brant for an inaugural presentation? It is nothardly an opera venue per se! Because of the unusual operatic nature of Krystyna's audition, the judges had concluded that she should be allowed two performances: the first would primarily focus upon 'expression' whilst the decisive performance would critically pay attention to her accuracy of musical sense:
She concluded the first evaluation to a surprising unenthusiastic bemused silence. She had unquestionably made her feelings felt and yet something in a particular way was missing: was her upper

register perhaps a little pinched at times? Had 'casta diva' ended rather abruptly? Was the whole aria spoiled by excessive vibrato?

Her initial performance was certainly weighed-up by uncertainty, confusion and the somewhat unqualified ignorance of us all.

She stood there watching and waiting, like some new flower beautiful and ready to be picked; whilst revered adjudicators and listeners alike cussed and noisily defamed all resolve. It was as though they were all in cahoots with insanity, each quarrelling to be heard yet not one person prepared to listen.

As for myself, I strived to hide behind their scorns and never uttered one word; it just seemed to me that so many no-nonsense and all-nonsense observations were being lambasted around that my viewpoint would not have held much water in any event.

Having said all that, it was my expressionless expression that said it all; combined with the realization that this young woman, whose name I couldn't rightfully recollect; had unknowing complicated and entangled every single important thing these venerable maestros had learned. That and the fact that her eyes were now screaming with tears and soddening the fur bib around her slight neck - that in its entirety most logically and pragmatically said it all for me!

In my hindsight I have learned how and why Krystyna's despairing tearfulness, actually became her saviour - and indeed would continue to be. Puzzling though it may seem, she was never knowing or aware that her vocalization required an emotional 'absence' of hope in order to bring about her deliverance - without the 'absence' she would be unimpassioned.

It was as though Krystyna was required to become empathetic to herself, thereby enabling her audience to become sympathetic to her. To whatever specific extent would be indefinable; enough to say that it is exclusively Krystyna's clandestine ability - it's everything she has and everything we wanted.

Scarcely into the second act the suppressed young woman from the sticks had almost miraculously metamorphosed into a fabled sophisticated actress. She really took no pity on us cretinous

4

creatures and simply delighted the entire forum with an operatic onslaught of pure and exacting prowess. The Brant reverberated - we were hooked and gawped dumbstruck as her diminutive figure faded into back-stage limbo - unarguably realizing we had been eye-witnessing genius.

Whatever peculiar inheritances, persuasions and perspectives regarding musical abilities that we had previously gathered, somewhere between Krystyna's upper notes and lower registers we needed to regroup that outmoded savvy!

Being endowed with the Krystyna 'experience' had left us all kind of enfranchised and overly smitten; that we had at least borne witness and 'gotten' the significance of the eloquent occasion. Although never could the so-called 'significantness' be lent an appropriate title - for me at least, it was merely as beguiling and as simplistic as prenatal signs; nothing more, nothing less!

The grapevine was a remarkable tool we possessed during those pre-IT simplistic decades, and it wasn't long into evening time that impresario Jacques Leyac breezed eagerly through from Montreal.

The sudden commotion and exploding flashbulbs suggested to me that this was no random visit!

Brant Inn Burlington Ontario

CHAPTER TWO

Flowers, Poems and Change

Why is it that 'change' can rarely define itself? Why does it frequently seem to have such an immense difficulty in succinctly expounding or to merely interpreting its precise nature? Yet given enough time 'change' can and will deliberately disturb and unpredictably alter the symmetry of permanence in literally everything and everybody.

Just when you were optimistically thinking that the ancient crack across the bedroom ceiling was lifeless and dormant, it unexpectedly awakens and begins to zigzag abruptly. Or just when the unfortunate little snail assumed it was quite safe to poke its head out of its wretched shell; it startlingly realizes that a huge predatory black bird has all along been following its tracks.

As likely as not, the truth of the matter is simply because no one has the ability any longer to listen and to hear the phenomenon of 'change' happening all around them. Or perhaps it is because they are hearing but unfortunately not really listening! Alas they have become so involved with their petty procrastinating that they are only able to process the adjectives that they deem are of relevance; or the more significant things of their choice.

The so-called irrelevant tiny single occurrences, such as a flower dropping its petals sadly and silently to the ground are far too wearisome to really care about. Yet how often do these irredeemable occurrences become so mightier and significant after they have happened and there is no turning back?

The after-wishes of Krystyna's evergreen dreams had become comparatively blurred of late. Conceivably they may have become slightly more troublesome to put together than the actual dream ever was. Although it was conspicuously apparent that this was the changing point of her vocation, the question that lingered was how could she get from here to out there successfully? Her whole life was littered by disappointment and even now she didn't dismiss failure as being a possibility; it was as though catastrophe had become her self-fulfilling prophecy in life.

However, Jacques Leyrac was thoroughly acquainted with all of those detrimental butterflies of the heart and furthermore he fully understood their origin. Jacques was a perfectionist who never grew impatient in his art of perfecting. Each and every precarious meter of the divide line between an artist's passion and their discovery of true perspective was beyond any doubt his specialty.

There is an instant interplay between a collective mass of human beings and a performer. It can be like a hymn to a kind of tribal rhythm and when its going well a unique transformation occurs that lifts the spirits to the Gods. Having said that, the call of the crowd can be as cruel as it is loving and can destroy a performer. Jacques realized the profound needs of all his apprehensive tenderfoots, and he provided it abundantly. It was as though he himself was the performer - a sole entity on a stage of self-assurance, a spotlight of eminence focused entirely upon him and no one else.

This was Jacques' impenetrable and somewhat arcane world in which there was no democracy, merely a sheer outshining dictatorship of direction. He made the ruling and everyone was better off for it.

In that long debunked world we all knew, all those distant decades ago, convention as we knew it hardly resonated in any serious manner to up and coming female entertainers; who aspired to sing operatic arias and such. In a male dominant society there was no overriding latitudes toward self-indulgent females; they either swim or they sink, it was as simple as that.

Perhaps therefore, it was not entirely super strange to observe that although Krystyna was undoubtedly the cause célèbre of immense jollification, it was also so paradoxically unseeming that she was being deliberately ignored. It was not as though they were intentionally cold-shouldering her - nearly all the guests paused momentarily and gave an obligatory 'hi'. However, as if they had predestined engagements they would move on quickly in order to hobnob with appreciably more influential "grown-ups".

Though it has to be said in his defence that the dynamic Mr Anderson had quite out of character abruptly requested a spray of red dahlias. He condescendingly snuffled to his dutiful concierge "for the wee girlie; - telephone Flowers & Fairy tales on Brant Street post haste"

Partway through all of the over-inflated congratulations and jubilations and at precisely the decisive pinpoint of sufficiency, Jacques began to semi-precipitously initiate his/their regretful farewells. He had detected that Krystyna was over-intoxicated by too many cream sodas and from his stand-point he had grown over tired by the pervasive invasion of bleached dentures and ballyhoo handshakes!

Names and numbers of the many illustrious unknowns began frantically to be exchanged upon the backs of beer mats and scribbled fallaciously upon own brand matchbook covers. There were several of the more discourteous freeloaders who were popping corks all over the place - the Brant became a curious establishment after Jacques' 'au revoir'!

I stood slightly captivated watching them both as they crossed the Brant's cobbled forecourt together toward Jacques' gleaming Lincoln Landau. It was as though I was trying my utmost to take in and memorize precisely how they both looked and every significant move they made. It was as though by some remarkable unknown intuition I was aware that someday, today would be immensely important to me again.

As I watched, Krystyna glanced back over her shoulder at all the well-wishers. Her Sunday stilettos must have caught in the small round stones and caused her to stumble slightly. She grasped in panic for Jacques' ever present arm and clung to it fast and rigorously. She more than realized that here was where she belonged. Like a novice nun in love with her God she was indeed the incomplete part of Jacques' spiritually orchestrated master plan. For me, I guess it was all part of an elaborate entertaining dream and perhaps some kind of divine confusion; I am still trying to decide!

Later on into that somewhat extreme evening, after the whole eventful shindig had fundamentally quietened down; I took the opportunity to loosen up a bit before my own evening show. No one appeared to think that I was "God-like"; sprawled out there on one of the Brant's enormous beige chesterfields in the lobby. But with a smoke between my fingers and a long envisaged beaker of espresso (first rate) for me it was pure heaven!

From this mere homeboy's perspective I was accordingly pretty much undaunted by all the unceremonious stream of out-of-towners who had abruptly descended on the Brant. Via the media maelstrom they had learned that something or someone significant was going-on and they didn't want to miss out!

It had all been kind of long and eventful for me and so I just lay there beneath my shades, people watching and trying to rummage together a poem in my addled brain. It wasn't going to be any type of smart rhyming poem, I guess it could be described as more in the nature of 'prosaic'! It was going to be along the lines of "missing the occurrence of a shooting star" etc etc. I dare to admit that is on the button of what came about today. Krystyna had come, dazzled us and disappeared - and all that we knew about her was zilch...particularly me; I would like to know what she likes to do on a Saturday evening or moreover, how to keep in touch! I was so much bewitched, bothered and bewildered that even the tiniest grain of enlightenment entirely one hundred per cent eluded me.

If you would try to imagine the unlikely hero in a "B" movie - the one between the cartoon and the main feature - odds are it really could be me! By such time that the hero gets the gall to get the gal the credits are beginning to roll!

And yet, almost inevitably, circumstances had a happy knack of working themselves out in those adolescent heydays of simplistic optimism. Together with every pipe dream that faded, a new one would undoubtedly grow in its place; although that useful sentiment was not something that I was conscious of at that time.

Later into that auspicious day a shipment of flowers were handed to the burly commissionaire in the lobby - principally carmine red dahlias. He in turn summoned a bellboy, who hightailed through to a housemaid, who lovingly arranged them into a vase and placed them back into the lobby. For several weeks or more they prettily enhanced the somewhat Gothic entrance as if it was an exquisite clearing in a forest.   And then one day, one by one the petals began to fall. It was as though they had some kind of certain sureness that sufficient time had elapsed and that Krystyna would not unexpectedly return to retrieve them.

Beauty as is often said lives mainly in the mind of the beholder - to some degree I have found that observation to be true, except when, of course, sensual expectations come into play.   For example, I once dated a dancer who insisted on wearing leg warmers under her clothes - said it was her concern for 'eased' muscles; but I'm not so sure! One day we got into undressing but by the time all that long underwear was removed the sensual expectations were somewhat dashed!

Although on the more positive side, I was once totally struck on our lay preacher's skinny daughter Sally-Ann-Jane. There was no doubt about it, I really did think she was the cat's pyjamas and the very least I could do was to wed her! And yet she had a prominent misshapen squint in her left eye, narrow sloping shoulders and well nigh no bust at all! I suppose the thing that attracted me to her the most was that I thought she was really 'cool' because she always seemed to dress in black - and carried a leather-bound prayer book! My mother said that Sally-Ann-Jane was a 'decent girl'; although I was uncertain precisely what mother meant by that.

Perhaps the truth is that neither of the previously mentioned companions were the persons I figured them out to be. And if you cross-reference that assumption with the way that they expected me to be, then it's no wonder it didn't work out for any of us.

Perhaps to some extent the way that we 'truthfully' are is not necessarily the way in which we like to portray ourselves - it differs from the way in which we desire people to perceive us.   I myself have tended to use my persona to suit the occasion. At times being somewhat ambiguous and obscuring who I am by substituting the person I want to be observed as.

A slightly typical example is my arrival on stage and particularly into the night club scene. It was obvious from the onset that half of me could be described as a reasonably "all right" singer; but what of the other half? The other half, the clever half, the significantly lied about half was just pure resilient Ham!

Now the low-down with being a hush-hush-ham is mainly to fully take on board that almost all of your audience are 'insentient' - or close to it! And that said, you don't strain your vocal cords for complete strangers who you will probably never entertain again and who haven't a clue whether your compositions contain two or four octaves!

I was once given some advice by a retired ex-trooper who said "a mongrel is far more intelligent than so-called pedigrees". If you believe that analogy of audience and performer then it becomes a sort of safety net of sorts to your own self-confidence. I would guess it's not that dissimilar to preferring to be an imaginary lover rather than a real one - it's by far safer in the long run!

All that said, I was still always kind of thrilled and sort of rekindled with a kind of optimism, when on a rare occasion a member of the audience has given a gift.

Once when I was hired as a wedding singer and after I had sung at the couples' levee for over two hours, the principal bridesmaid gave me an enormous pumpkin pie as a thank you. At another somewhat raucous function someone unknown threw me a pair of 'weed-in' knickers - bet that never happened to Elvis!

But the most captivating and endearing gift that I have ever received was left for me anonymously. I had been employed to sing romantic ballads at a ruby anniversary celebration. During the interval I discovered that a single red rose had been left for me in the dressing room. The inscription read simply "To Ricky; roses are the flowers of love".

If Proust himself maintained that "genius consists in its powers of reflection and not necessarily in the intrinsic quality of the performance" then who am I to disagree?

I hope that my intentions are becoming a little clearer to you, in as much that the wish-wash regarding my personal involvement hasn't sidetracked the story for you. I guess that I am endeavouring to draw some king of analogy between the somewhat ridiculous clandestine concoctions of my life, versus the consummate instinctiveness of Krystyna's life.

From the very first moment the curtain rose she would begin to command the source of your soul; like some Louisiana evangelist. It was startling how she always gave the impression that she was looking directly at you and singing directly to you - it would make you go all red outside and in. I remember that I didn't like it that much the first time she did it, and yet I didn't half wish she'd do it again!

The very essence of Krystyna's performance was her acting, it seemed to be almost schizophrenic by nature. In her role she became somebody else; never herself; in every respect the character she portrayed was not imaginary.

The dilemma of it all is the occupational hazard of only the most masterly of operatic singers who are able to refine the gift of fantasy until it becomes a kind of professional pretence. Many of them succeed, by finding along the way a core of themselves that is kept secret and in a sense is hallowed and untouched by the disguises. Others like Krystyna take years before they finally learn that their lives have been wrapped in an illusion. An illusion that has to be torn away like so many layers of an onion skin before they can find true freedom again.

For the better part of almost a week I tried ineptly to wrap up the 'Shooting Star' poem I had been working on. Not being able to get to grips with it at all was really beginning to irritate me and virtually complicating my days schedule. Come what may that noxious poem never did materialize for me. I suppose that the reason for my extraordinary ineptitude to compose a simple poem was because it was about Krystyna. I just wanted everyone from Montreal to Munich to get it! Perhaps there are some experiences that cannot be shared and some aspirations that are just too complicated to share!

However, it was those 'left behind' dahlias of Krystyna's that finally got me out of the doldrums with myself. They put me in mind of part of a Myrtiotissa verse which translated reads:

"here before your feet, I scatter full of longing,
        the rich-petaled blossom of my life'

A sentiment especially for the dahlias or/and Krystyna perhaps?

Small things of little or no consequence mattered quite a lot to Krystyna. Like for instance an enormous ginger tom cat (of some age and considerable experience) who had mastered the fungi roof tiles and impudently tiptoed through her open bedroom window. It was late one Sunday afternoon when he arrived and apparently he kept her company until sunset (she said) and then somewhat leisurely he climbed back out. He had a soft Cheshire cat smile (she said).

And so you see it really <u>did</u> matter a lot to Krystyna whether or not the elderly gentleman who was driving Jacques Leyrac's splendid Lincoln really was his actual chauffeur. Although (according to Jacques) his driver's title was open to some speculation (or conjecture) it really was of great momentous importance for Krystyna to be knowing.

Jacques tried to close the conversation by informing her "he is just an old pal who happens to like wearing Brando caps" and as though he half realized that the explanation was not sufficiently adequate he subtly added "either way Max will take us all home safely - and he always has the good sense to know exactly where that is".

It seems to me that so-called creative folks in show business are somewhat dependent upon regular folk like Max, and of course the converse is also true. It is as though they both function like "family" of opposites and can genuinely become kind of 'lost' without an off beat mix of one another. In any event that was how I interpreted Jacques' perception of Krystyna's dubiety at that time. Back in Montreal the bloodhounds were out and yelping in anticipation of Krystyna's imminent arrival. Jacques had gotten a tip-off that several Hollywood style interviews had out of the blue been given the thumbs up without his endorsement. To some extent it was beginning to become complicatedly out of Jacques' sensible control; and he did not like that!

On account of all the impending rumpus and the lack of etiquette Jacques tactically decided to curtail Krystyna's launch - for at least the short term

Jacques had watched it all happen many times and for that reason he had a very different perspective on so-called show business; he certainly was not the traditional 'Mr Big'. In Jacques' view there had to be a distinct separation between the entertainer and ragamuffins (the press). Otherwise such a potpourri of illusionary influences would come into play and most of them would be embellished poppycock. Theirs was a prepaid indulgence of farcical charade, a make-shift idolization which in the real world was the media's dionysiac tribute to the immensity of their own phallus - and nothing more besides! Although Jacques had a good working relationship with the aforementioned 'opportunists' he preferred to preserve a certain 'mystique' with regard to his wards. "Too much limelight can have an adversive effect" he maintained.

He once told me "Judy Garland is dead and everyone took her eventual suicide for granted - as a way of life!" "Remember, you've got to Ac-cent-tchu-ate the positive; eliminate the negative. (Johnny Mercer). That way you'll know for sure that they are killing you, and you can STOP!!! If you really put your mind to it!

Jacques felt that it was his prerogative to discourage her from too much virtuosity; but only for the purpose of unravelling how unreality looks in realist terms. However, as luck would have it Krystyna was oblivious to her virtuosic prowess in any event, and that's all any of us desired.

Jacques had scheduled Krystyna in to lodge with his widowed sister Ernestine for several weeks. She lived in a spacious solid brick built house at the end of Chestnut Street in downtown Toronto. It was a well-maintained and handsome property in a decent neighbourhood - it was also considered as being the 'second best' Century home in that local.

Krystyna enjoyed it a lot; living there with Ernestine. She particularly looked forward to the weekends when Jacques would travel in from Montreal and they were all together. From time to time Jacques and Ernestine would dance to Strauss around and around the sitting room; it was quite a marvel to watch them both. Their motions were more fluid than liquid neon and even though the floor was crowded with furniture, not one step of theirs was ruined.

It was only a few days off Christmas and Krystyna was unusually over-excited and in top form. She tiptoed slightly apprehensively into the sitting room looking exceedingly mischievous in order to join Ernestine for supper. Like a marionette with some loquacious tale to tell she just kind of hung there until Ernestine had given her full attention. "I really am the most strangest person in the whole world Ernestine, because I have been born several times over don't you know". Seemingly the background to Krystyna's frivolous remark was due to an article she had read in the 'Metro' which claimed she was born in Poland of Catholic parentage. In contrast the 'Star' were claiming that she was a second generation Protestant Canadian! Krystyna's expression saddened. "Just before Mama died I asked her if we belonged here; she simply replied that a sailor man had brought us here. Perhaps I was born on the immigrant vessel?"

Ernestine shook her head in annoyance and dizzy disbelief "It's so scandalous the way in which the press make assumptions. It seems to me that your sudden fame has left them all kind of bewildered, and now all and sundry are just competing to be knowledgeable about you". She added jestfully "they are all loony my dear; it's enough to make even Mary Baker Eddy question her denomination and birthplace!"

Not one novena or silent night was sung for either Jacques, Ernestine or Krystyna during those nippy nativity weeks of 1959. Indeed why would they wish for such when they clearly possessed all they could ever desire; here in each other.

Bright poinsettias and red ribbons tied to cedar and pine and ample armfuls of amazing predilection. Krystyna's lifetime of longing for this epitome of unique closeness was almost near to addiction, and she knew it!

CHAPTER THREE

Familiar Strangers

Why is it that it's always the strangers in life that do us the most good and regrettably the most harm. Not necessarily the people that we see on the streets or in passing, cars, or mirrored in shop windows, but moreover it's the people who we think we understand and who seemingly understand us; yet in reality we have no inkling about one another at all. These are often the stalwarts in our life, the people who candidly and confidently assure us that they will always be there - and then suddenly and quite unexpectedly they disappear. And gradually as all the lights dim into darkness there only remains a deafening silence, as though some huge clocking-out book has finally been closed. Perhaps it is these people who tend to unwillingly complicate our lives and consequently they are conceivably making us a tiny bit more sceptical after each new encounter.

If somewhat nostalgically I cover my drowsy eyes and allow angel wings to transport my thoughts through to 1959/61; it seems as though quite miraculously the injurious past may somehow have been resolved. Although wishful thinking has always been my forte and it is more likely that the legacy of those years has merely been comatosed. In which case it is presently beginning its journey forward - quite predominantly so!

Here, on the other side of time it is easy to glance at the past subjunctively; although it is somewhat difficult to figure out how all of those who crossed my path could have somehow gotten a slightly healthier deal. Precisely what they needed was another season. One that they could neatly wedge between winter and spring. It could have been a season of ostensible soul-searching and reproachable reflection. A season where absolutely no one can fall and only learn their lesson after they have landed.

To the following beautiful strangers and foolhardy strangers whomsoever, I cheerfully dedicate an unused season to you:-

17

Charles Hardin Holly, Richard Valens and The Big Bopper who in January 1959 crashed on take-off from an Iowa airport. All died. I recollect growing my hair ridiculously long afterwards, perhaps in a effort to resolve and deal with the outrage of it all. Did the music die? I have no conclusion.

John Murray Anderson was rumoured to be leaving the Brant after 37 years. It was the spring of '61 and the majority of us paid no heed to the tittle-tattle. However, a couple of years on and the Brant was purchased by a Toronto Corporation who tore it down for a hotel/apartment complex that never did materialize.

"Kim Denisa (former Krystyna Comanescu) has regrettably quit my stable" - press release via impressario Jacques Leyrac; September 9th 1961 quite ruffled and feeling antagonized by an obtrusive press her unrehearsed response was "I'm perfectly capable of scooting across the road safely without Mr Leyrac!"

The unsympathetic way in which the news was knitted together and reported still vexates me; although most of the teen fanzines were compassionate to her.

Meyer Lansky was finally breezed away from Canada with a helping hand of the RCMP. However, Charles (Lucky) Luciano died suddenly of a heart attack - after gulping down a cup of coffee, or so they say.   Together they were instrumental in setting the Organization down the road in an organized way; yet circa '61 was unluckily nothardly their most advantageous year.

It becomes comparatively difficult to describe in precise details the complicit calibre of the various mythical mirages in sharp suits who intermittently dropped in on the Limberlost. Both Bliss and Mom deemed it somewhat beneficial to remain neighbours of the brotherhood, way after 1933 when prohibition was finally repealed. In spite of that, what puttered across Mom's brow most frequently was how it was a damned travesty of justice that her ingenious invention never once was bought to fruition prior to the '33 repeal: to wit a mighty powerful cocktail chaser to disguise the mighty foul taste of Meyer et al illicit Whisky!

I visited Mom just before Christmas during '61. As I pulled onto the restaurant forecourt she was giving some fellas in a huge black limo a friendly wave goodbye. I remember thinking how unusual it was; a vehicle of that excellence out here in this neck of the woods. Mom rambled on about how at Christmas even children pray to Santa Claus and that those fellas were just early Santa's with a sack or two of judgments that they'd been sent to deliver. That evening, little by little I began to fundamentally take on board the provenance of those aloof gentlemen. Although the exact nature of their work was not entirely crystal clear to me, I guess I got the gist of it. When I tactfully broached Mom with regard to her role in the conspiratorial enterprise she just unpretentiously spelled it out for me: "one of our Almighty's most gratifying creations is sacrificed to fulfil the law - and it really wasn't his fault! Why in the name of justice should I have mercy upon every man jacks liver when they know darn well that booze is truly the disease that purports to cure everything. At least on the other side of the coin someone makes a buck or two - is that really so bad, particularly during these hard times?" I guess that Mom always did prefer to paddle her own canoe and chart her own course for that matter!

Returning to the unused season, mentioned several paragraphs ago - for clarification:-

Don't you agree that it's somewhat bizarre and therefore, curiously interesting how in all of the instances mentioned, the individuals involved all appear to interlink exceedingly well? For example, although each individual is totally dispensable to another they are never-the-less (non-envisaged) compatible strangers. In as much that each 'stranger' is over-capable of performing acts of immense creative imagination, rather than being in a conventional somewhat passive arena in which all ideas interact mechanistically?

"IF A MAN COULD PASS THROUGH PARADISE IN A DREAM, AND HAVE A FLOWER PRESENTED TO HIM AS A PLEDGE THAT HIS SOUL HAD REALLY BEEN THERE, AND IF HE FOUND THAT FLOWER IN HIS HAND WHEN HE AWOKE - AYE, AND WHAT THEN?"

Samuel Taylor Coleridge
(Anima Poetae)

Perhaps when it all boils down everyone owns a diamond ring - diamanté, zirconium or otherwise. And everyone has some Sunday shoes, a necktie or two and a tony petticoat. Maybe even a Pennsylvania Pistol in the back of the closet?

CHAPTER FOUR

'Chiaroscuro' for Renek

As far as can be ascertained it could be interpreted that possibly his incessantly procrastinating conscience had finally gotten the better of his heart-searching in the end. Unless that is, he possibly had some sort of Zen metamorphose; particularly in view of the fact that the tag-end of his life was obviously approaching fast. In any event too much of his time had been wasted away watching and worrying for that elusive shadow that might quickly sneak underneath the door. Perhaps now, if only for salvation purposes he was due to receive just a smidgen of God's magnanimousness, or even a teensy-weensy benefit of the doubt would not go amiss.

Although there is a train of thought that suggests that purely the consequences of those awful ill-conceived actions have of late instigated his hidden conscience. And that without the reminder of those unpleasant consequences, his of late conscience would never have come into play? When all is said and done conscience vs consequence can be just a duck and dive Gideon for quick-witted zealots who are more than familiar with the ingeniousness of such systematic methods. In other words, to ante-up all of your diminished integrity and responsibility by interfusing a confession with Bibles of excessive unctuousness is nothardly compassionately noble, but a good idea nevertheless!

Notwithstanding that the inappropriate misappropriation of trust cannot hardly be viewed as a wicked/evil hamstringing offence in any event, can it? Although a synergy of trust must have existed in the first place - and that is obviously also open to question, whether it was or not? It seems to me that if some sort of synergy did exist and suddenly its let slip, then fortuitously a whole smorgasbord of wilful and obnoxious shenanigans will kick in.

How peculiar it is, how strangers who have congratulated each other in sharing the same fears of loneliness and pain, also share the same disregard to cruelty when inflicting it. Oh, holy short-short-sightedness through lovelorn eyes should rarely be devalued in a wise world - but it wasn't wise was it?

Be all that as it may, what now of the dark parenthesis of punishment and how do we administer it? Should punishment be somehow punitive to the so-called crime? Or perhaps it should be retributive to the suffering it has defiley caused? It seems logical that in the first instance (creation say) our almighty Lord has already provided us with such eclectic answers in the many outlines of 'his' great utopia. For example, if the Almighty deems it is necessary for both the Godless and also the God-fearing to don identical moustaches and funny clothes - not mention our almost rigorously apocryphal facial expressions - it is most probably likely because he reasoned that when all the chips have been counted most of his creations are divinely imperfectiously flawed. Somewhere in the heavenliness of production there was a mess-up of muchness, and as luck would later dictate, there was no going back to the drawing board. Except perhaps to entangle each homo sapien entity with filled to the brim moral tracts of reference - should they need it! To wit: In reasoning that the creation was ultra presumptive by fault, and that because of this high-minded and unfortunately individualized perspective (didactically influential to us) we are all-powerfully imbalanced from the very onset of life. Add to this scripture several ambiguously unwarranted rules and uncompromising theisms, and it seems clear that Renek Comanescu (poor soul) was damned and accursed since Genesis!

Although conscience/consequence is seldom an animality we possess, it can be brought about nevertheless in shed loads of similar (or dissimilar) forms. In Renek's situation it was entirely a case of 'resignation'. All of the fussy esoteric reasoning, decades of aberrant perseverance, just to stay alive, he was plain bone-tired with all of it. Always attempting to second-guess Le Parrain was not a masquerade that he wanted to put-on indefinitely - he was growing too weary of all of that two steps ahead double-dealing. Renek was fully aware that he had been an embarrassingly conspicuous (and elusive) damp patch on Le Parrain's wall for far too lengthy a period. He knew that the borrowed days had become fewer and now it was pay back time.

Silence, remoteness, wisdom, power: these are the essential watchwords that govern the behaviour of Le Parrain. Quite apart from close members of his family there were rumours even on the streets that Le Parrain had been dishonoured by the disappearance of Renek.

And only the ray of Le Parrain lucidity could penetrate, colder and colder and without mercy, any doubt, any hope, any shiver and restore the status quo ecstatically on a silver tray once and for all. They had searched through fields and fields of haystacks looking for that elusive needle but now the end was almost nigh, at long last the clothes line maze between tenement and Erie Pinelands had grown almost threadbare; this was the point in time where everyone's broken dreams and memories meet, this was finality exquisite.

That cherished timberland home that seemed to hug the landscape and felt so distant and safe from the external world. That yesterday of yearning; and of the perdition when all of the singing stopped dead, as though the words were irretrievable. In fact, there never were any words after Krystyna was gone.

It seems now that Evelyn Levine's vignette of Renek's prognosis may indeed have a ring of truth about it. Perhaps it was the fever and delirium that finally betrayed him and not necessarily his conscience per se? Or perhaps it was all much of a muchness when all was said and done.

He'd walked all the roads there were to walk and some there never were. He'd seen all the towns there were to see but never discovering in any of them the valuables that he'd left behind. He himself in the final termination had concluded that the distance of doggedness had outrun his fortitude. Broken finger posts and lamented friends were the only assurances the world could offer him; it was too late to expect anything else.

The sky above the city had darkened some. If there was any where for a pilgrim to find shelter it wasn't letting on. Renek could easily feel all of his watchwords liquefying as though even they had had enough. The air was frigid with want, the rain ambivalent as it filtered through his clothing; the signals were all there, non-rescindably explicit and he realized it. Just a pre-established unkind example of nature stepping in and taking her course. An unvarying preamble of the throngs of death: where past and present are virtually inextricable, where nothardly any prayerful plea can bring about release - excepting repentance and the ultimate release.

The day in which he died was the best day he could remember. He had waited for it, prayed for it, wanted to jump the queue ahead of anyone else who may have had desires on his day. He had once written a poem in his own blood when he was a young man back in Poland. Yes, real blood warm and red and addressed to those loud-mouthed politicians who forever waste the blood of others. He remembered thinking it'll find readers - at least he hoped so. And now the time has come, at last, to finish the poem. Now, right now (just a little longer, a moment more, just let me begin it, just let me end it.)

At first though the wind, followed by the heavy rain in earnest as Renek smashed to the sidewalk. And then very soon the nigh-on faerie footsteps harkening slow and steady down the concrete street; away, away. And just for one decisive negligible instant he recalled 'her' who he had left behind and he finished that poem... And then zip, the predicable full stop on overdue family business.

That's just the way that it all finally worked out for Renek Comanescu; a transpiration of beautiful clinical sublimity in its extreme form. Just unbefittingly prior to evensong around late December in 1958; Renek Comanescu received his overdue prescribed medicament. There were no medals for this Freedom Fighter, just a gift of guarantee for his daughter.

A gift of supreme guardianship so special that it would transcend and outshine the barrel of the gun that slayed him. Krystyna Comanescu would have a family. She was their neophyte and they would educate her magnificently.

Renek had always been her bastardized rainbow to nowhere, the parent that insentiently she found was so necessary to believe in when she knew inwardly it was pointless to do so. His undeviating mood, his unalterable expression they were all for her all of the time and yet they were as well all power for the course of ineffectual hopelessness. And she the immortal snowbird who he so ineptly and brilliantly destructively fed with his bitter crumbs of comfort from the chafed wounds in his entrusted hands. And who he hastily shooed away when his hands grew uselessly empty. Foolhardy mistakes. Long-lasting nefarious misunderstandings, so many unaccountable disasters. A befuddled bequeathment of iniquity to pass on to any child. And yet perhaps in an introspective way Renek had bestowed her with a kind of extreme equilibrium. Perhaps now in Krystyna's own revolutions she will be able to find a touch so vibrantly unique to change all that needs to change in a persons heart and in hers as well.   A touch that cannot be taught; a touch that has to be experienced in full to be appreciated.

Krystyna's unknown benefactor was reported to be the third highest payer of taxes in Southern Ontario. Outwardly an extremely respectable businessman; albeit his business interests were kind of surreptitious in nature. Nevertheless, several random checks by the CRA (Canada Revenue Agency) had processed nothing untoward. I guess he gave them a pain where a pill can't reach, however, it was a legitimate irritation and that's all that mattered.

He was a kind of remote individual - not in an irrelevant sense; perhaps more like a poker player who is hedging his bets. His equerry once disclosed to me that Le Parrain enjoyed reading the obituaries out loud - said it was his way of ascertaining where the dead lived and whether the dead lived and why the dead lived, if indeed they do!

It's so super-strange how every Tom, Dick, Harry and Pete have their personalized opinionated arguments regarding Le Parrain. If you permit them to yak they'll even invent some arguments you may never have heard of before. Just for once in a while I would really like to listen to some brand new positive and enthusiastic ovations for Le Parrain and perhaps even a few constructive questions about him. Like for instance how/why did he manage to thwart the sanctimonious city fathers from tearing down the dilapidated old tenement blocks across my street? The elderly lady who still inhabits the block, still sits on her cushions high behind her flower boxes on the 7th floor. So are the hop-scotch lines on the cracked sidewalk outside, It is as though that little neck of the woods has been infused with a magical force-field right around the perimeter.

I once read where he was quoted as saying that he advocated severe capital punishment for drivers who carelessly and rancorously run over rabbits and squirrels. And purgatory at the very least for those repugnant individuals who drive into dogs and cats.

It seems to me that sort of sobriety to one-liners is deserving of an accolade. Supposedly his less intimidating one-liner was "leave them guessing like Durante would" - in deadly detail, whatever it takes, he unequivocally has that proficiency all wrapped up in bundles.

CHAPTER FIVE

'Commingle'

Jacques Leyrac had lived alone for far more years than he cared to remember; although it was by choice it hadn't always been that way. In spite of the positivity he had been blessed with, he still found it impossible (and well nigh impracticable) to open up his heart to even the most ardent admirer. Jacques was determined not to let even a little-bitty hurt to infiltrate his armour and the person who taught him the value of such was Le Parrain - an associate of time-honoured cognizance. It was this abiding relationship that was an important consideration when quite unexpectedly Jacques was invited to lunch with the ageing compatriot. So many bitter winters had passed since they had broken bread together, to make Jacques realize that something of an unusual nature was afoot.

During their adolescent years the two of them used to hang-out together. Le Parrain had often been somewhat cruel and emotionally humiliating in his judgements and comments on Jacques developing career with showbizzy types. "Why do it" he would ask. Jacques didn't realize it then but his companion was 'en-route' to the choices of his elders, and in a way he was harshly judging himself for not having had the courage to say "NO" to them.

Shortly after Le Parrain's advancement and undoubtedly in a effort to evince and thereby exert his freshly secured supremacy; he politely 'requested' Jacques to persuade a certain Can-Can dancer from the Moulin Rouge to 'stop-by', Jacques was reasonably sure that it wouldn't be anything of that complexion again!

It was a beautiful mid-summer's evening when Jacques journeyed out to Lake Cartier to rendezvous with Le Parrain. It was pretty much dark by the time he arrived and the moon had scattered a path wide enough to be a highway across the surface of the lake. There seemed to be an infinite number of people out there that night. Some sitting on benches, some lounging on the grass, others were just standing and looking into the water. A man in 'dress' shorts with a blow up dinosaur under his arm greeted Jacques with a firm handshake and escorted him to Le Parrain majestic maisonette on the top floor.

In contrast to the lazy mood down beside the lake there was a somewhat grandiose dinner party sessioning at Le Parrain retreat. A white-gloved lackey beeline instinctively toward Jacques and showed him to his seat next to a huge smiley lady; dusted his lap with a serviette and poured him a tall heady Bellini in English crystal - French Champagne though!

'Le Parrain had a penchant for these type of elaborate rituals, albeit from a somewhat borrowed culture that did not fundamentally parallel his own. He would preside over at the head of the table. Women were bedecked with jewels, men in tuxedos. As likely as not the dishes on fire, and sometime sooner or later a cavalcade of desserts and enormous cheeses served on great platters.

All this would usually be topped off by demitasse and inbided in the two living rooms; one for the men and one for the women. The sexes mixed again late, after the men's agenda had been dealt with. There was no dope, no cocaine. There was no marijuana. There was instead booze, the luxury of opulence and the dependability that every man-jack would rigorously endorse Le Parrain pronouncement and thus be rewarded for their support.

By a mixture of fear and charm, Le Parrain came to hold all of those monkey suits in thrall. He divided and ruled them - and in the end he took their mindsets over completely.

<u>The discourse 'twixt Jacques Leyrac and Le Parrain (recast for the general reader in English)</u>

"Remember those one-night stands we used to do Jacques? Getting changed in the back of an Oldsmobile; the performers travel and sleep in buses nowadays Jacques. Have you seen them? The buses are like luxurious hotel rooms with double beds, wet bars and TV. Do you remember going to that party at Chico Fernadnez house? I walked into the host's bedroom and put my coat on top of all the others piled on the bed. Someone moved underneath. A small dark-haired fella smiled at me. It was Sal Mineo. Sad about how he was killed wasn't it? You were the best cleffer around in those days Jacques, no one had your style... And you've done so well! Now I need your assistance, I need you to take charge of and oversee a particular situation that is extremely personal to me.

Every wise-guy these days is into some kind of mental masturbation but in reality Jacques they cannot tell the difference between a fancy coffin and an ottoman in the hall; it's all the same to them Jacques, but you and I know there is a difference don't we? Life it too subjunctive nowadays: the days are past when you could just call up Colonel Sanders and a pair of goons - give Joe Blow a ruptured testicle and a bloody nose and get the fuck out of it!

There's guys now Jacques who do not have as much as a seat in their pants who are doing larceny and punishment murders; there's no damned correlation Jacques, but by and large they're doing well.

Anyhow Jacques I would never offer you anything of an unethical nature. In the fewest possible words I merely want you to nurture a certain young woman for me. Strengthen her Jacques; I have a long-standing hope for her and I would be mercifully grateful to you." Jacques looked long and hard into his compadre's eyes "when these questions are done and finally answered I hope they'll not be asked again". "They won't be Jacques" he firmly replied.

The descriptive disclosure 'twixt Jacques and Le Parrain

"She' is not your average chorine Jacques, she will boff you to bits if you let her, so be certain you build a strong fence around her real quick. The moment you see her running, stop her Jacques. She has no idea of the aspirations worth stopping for unless you make them evident to her.

She needs to string out her terpines in your shadow Jacques. That is the only way that true reality will begin for her - your shadow will make her real or reality without you will turn her into a shadow of no-one."

Jacques honourably kissed Le Parrain out stretched hand, thanked him and took his leave.

Usually there's a pretty good reason for giving a greenhorn artist a particularly more suitable name. It might be that the promoter is named Joe and so his prodigy may end up being called Joanne, or in the Southern United States where they invent such beautiful first names she might be given a compromise of Joline, Jody or Joe-Mae. My father was a great Crosby fan, fortunately, I wasn't named Bing, when I first took to the boards - that would have been a tough act for me to follow! However, Jacques decided to keep Krystyna's name 'evident' (to him) and 'easily understood' (again to him). Her name would be "Kim" - (no distinctive surname) - like Cher or Ann-Margaret. It was a name that gave him solace, a far off name where distance hasn't changed. A name where his watch ran slow and he could remove himself from real time and avidly recall the warmth two minutes before his beloved wife's breath abruptly stopped.

Jacques performed his obligations to Le Parrain et al to the letter and beyond. He devised Kim's scripts, cleverly included her ripostes and created her public persona. It was all a continuous process of balancing, judging, altering and refining. This was for Jacques the artfulness that made the whole process so absorbing; to start with the 'general' and to end up with the sublimely 'particular'.

Although there were some occasions when he became fearful that perhaps he'd molly-coddled her a good deal more than he should have, and that she might waiver or worse still 'freeze'. But it never happened whilst she was underpinned by Jacques. Kim recognized that to some degree she was Jacques' marionette, that he was working the strings but at the same time she was creating the magic that the onlookers would rise to.

Kim had once confided in me that Jacques was her masterly knight errant, slaying every dragon and horrible face tree that dwelt in the forest and making every single thing wholesome and perfect for her. Without a doubt they really were the most sensational confederates and whether they were awakened to it or not, particular tenderness for one another was also furtively emerging.

Although he had taught her many times to speak his lines, he on the other hand was speaking volumes of uncertainty to himself.

For the foremost time in Jacques loquacious lifetime he had begun to cross-question his integrity; "am I now nearer to whatever Kim wants or expects" he rummaged ungracefully "or am I far than nothing and it's only me who expects?"

CHAPTER SIX

View with a grain of sand

Jacques knew of only one boarding school in Southern Ontario with an established and reputable conservatoire and there was only one good teacher who was worth her weight in gold who worked there. She was enthusiastic about Kim and immediately took her on as a pupil.

It should be mentioned that there were not an abundance of respected institutions which produced the world's leading opera singers at that time, and hence there were very few teachers who had the ability to realize the enormous potential of a pupil. Little needed be said about Luigiana Scicolone, for posterity will scarcely remember her name; yet it was her who discovered Kim's real voice. Luigiana too had been a lyric soprano and had sang at the Royal Alex on Yonge Street for years, prior to her being pensioned off. The problem was that as she got older she got plump, and although her voice was still flawless her presence on stage was not impressive for an 'evolved' generation.

Luigiana recognized that beneath Kim's placid exterior there was a lava boiling in her that was waiting to explode into life. They embarked on a course of intensive lessons and vocal exercises, Luigiana enjoining Kim's efforts, her instructive voice just trembling with emotion. It was to be the summertime of Kim's life - a place set aside for her by Carmen, Lucia, Santuzza and God.

There is no one I know of who can shed enough light on what it was like to witness Kim's astonishing premiere performance in front of the entire school. And therefore, I find it unachievable to try my hand at attesting a scenario that couldn't in all honesty be the accurate truth - perhaps the learned readers version of inexplicability would be all that is required. But hell, what does it matter in any event, when we every bit have the facts to validate it!

All these years later when we listen to recordings of Kim's voice on the radio we have perhaps grown somewhat complacent and accustomed to that prestigious voice; but what of those beautifyingly garnished notes of joy/bottomless despair; what must it have been like for those privileged few who heard her for the first time, that long-ago evening in 1958?

I thought at the time it was a somewhat bizarre role for her to play, that of Violetta; however, in retrospect she never acted any other role as fully - deliberately singing in such a weak and broken voice, because 'dear' Violetta in act III is weak and broken. In many respect she lived the role as she acted it in later life.

Although it was entirely Kim's own disastrous decision to employ the manipulatively renowned Leroy Strooduhs as her manager, she could never have envisaged that he would systematically 'crush' her.

I recall how Leroy had an almost pathological addiction to wearing expensive and ostentatious shoes. After a dog walker saw Leroy's body floating in Lake Ontario, his snazzy shoes were being washed up on the Lake shore for several months afterwards! I retrieved one of his winkle-picker shoes amongst some flotsam, dried it out and kept it on my mantle for quite a few years. They say that the great lake always gives up its dead. I've often thought how strange that saying is. For example, although Leroy's body went straight to the bottom of the lake it wasn't that long before it popped up again off Burlington Beach. Kind of ironic too how his body was heading toward the Brant!

Undigress to Kim's haunting rendition of Violetta; her essential role circa '58. Connect that same rendition with an irreverent graphic annotation, e.g.: the skinniest, spotty faced girl with mega enormous bifocals... She squinting, lost and seemingly alone; we goggle eyed in disbelief! She stole our hearts that evening and if I could shed any semblance of light of what it was like to witness Kim's premiere performance then I would; but I can't! It seems to me there are some facets of wonder where only God is permitted, we all found them that amazing evening and we all wilfully trespassed!

CHAPTER SEVEN

De Goils!

The scene was the entrance to a nightspot. Enter Mae West magnificently dripping in jewellery. Cries the hat-check girl: "Goodness! What lovely diamonds!" Mae West, cigarette dangling from her sultry lips: "Goodness...had nothing to do with it...dearie"

It was never really openly established just what kind of dame Mae West was playing in that 1930's George Raft movie, but with all those rocks she looked like the gangster's moll to top them all. Those gorgeous screen dames, they seemed to live out their lives in long, clinging satin "negligees", drank gin by the bath-tub load, got knocked about and had an amazing ability to throw hair-brushes and plates.

But the truth was far more unsurpassed than the fiction could take on board - the <u>real</u> incisive and punchy ladies of that era were the Polly Adler's, Clark Barkers and Bliss Provenzano - to name but a few.

The times were reshaping, adjusting, channelling into unfamiliar territory. Prohibition was repealed at the end of 1933; boot-legging as big business had its limitations, and Al Capone was on his way to jail for income-tax evasion. There were many "Get in, Bud. You're going for a ride" guys that no one wanted any longer and there were even many so-called legitimized organizations who were being dragged down by the ineptness and venality of those around them. Yet some of the more 'consolidated' establishments managed to win through. Bliss Provenzano was comfortably consolidated and she wound through with relative ease.

Joseph Kennedy became the American distributor of Haig & Haig Whisky and Gordon's Gin. Frank Costello set up Alliance Distributors, selling the same brands he'd made popular illegally. Samuel Bronfman, the biggest Canadian bootlegger founded a company called Seagrams and 'Bugsy' Siegel started up Capital Wine and Spirits - which specialized in top-end wines and

Liqueurs. Bliss just took a leaf or so out of prohibitions major players book and in her own impetuous fashion she 'also' went into legitimate business. And with a noteworthy favour from Monsieur Bronfman regarding improvements to her 'horse-and-buggy' still, and to her felonious proscription it was fait accompli for her all the way.

Principally Bliss' new direction was not only to make certain that her long established hop-heads were entirely satisfied with her post prohibition hooch, but also that in this 'dry' area it would appeal to a wider and new generation of incomers. Unlike in the flavourful prohibition era Bliss realized the importance of avoiding pernicious 'top-ups' of methylated substances and such like, or 'spill-overs' as she liked to discreetly refer to them!

Moreover, she also had a need to breathe new life into her reputation. The opinions and beliefs that were generally held about her were somewhat noisome in nature of late. "Keep in with the rogues and the honest folk wont hurt you". In matters of public-spiritedness and of dipsomania this would become her new by-word. En passant, in Bliss' estimation "the rogues" were the provincial police. She had invariably figured on hanging on to some of the old traditions, there was just no point in dismissing their usefulness. Withal the OPP's always had been invaluable custodians to the Limberlost basement - they held the key and Bliss was downright obliged that they did. It always seemed to me that Bliss was at least one skedaddle ahead of them in any event; I guess that was her true forte!

CHAPTER EIGHT

De Goils and De Guys

Rico was standing in front of his mirror, combing his hair with a little ivory pocket comb. Rico was vain of his hair. It was black and lustrous, combed straight back from his low forehead and arranged in three symmetrical waves.

Rico was a simple man. He loved but three things: himself, his hair and his gun. He took excellent care of all three:-

One chapter from 'Little Caesar'

The weather in downtown Toronto that spring afternoon of 1938 was sultry, foreshadowing the heat of summer. Over at Fran's Restaurant on St. Clair the important business of selecting the evening's dinner menu was just beginning. The manager of the restaurant Nicolai Dostolevsky stepped out of his office, walked through the two dining rooms onto the street and was never seen or heard of again. His assistant later recalled that Nicolai had taken a telephone call just prior to leaving, at around 4:35pm.

Nicholai Dostolevsky was undoubtedly a character who lived out of his time; several hundred years before, he would have been a robber baron whose descendants would today be totally respectable members of some European aristocracy. But unfortunately for him he just happened to be born in 1895 not 1195.

Sure, Nikolai was one of a kind, if the organization every had glamour, then it was he who first injected it; dressing with fedora and silk suit and such. There was however, a paradoxical incongruity because Nikolai Dostolevsky was not ever a sophisticated big-shot businessman or for that matter neither was he a big-shot hood. There was no contradiction in the assumption that he liked to believe in his own savoir faire, however, beneath the tuxedos breathed a dungareed redneck, callous thug and an erstwhile escaped convict.

But the times really were changing and wise operators were already turning to new and revolutionary methods of obtaining a dishonest buck without having to terrorize an honest citizen in doing it. 'Image', - the impression of a person or organization to the public had become an important factor of late. The organization as such, no longer themselves had any direct involvement in crime of any kind. Instead it was only through their intermediaries that so-called profits were laundered and only through the most legitimate businesses in the world.

It was for sure that an organization that was not allied to crime per se, was more likely to be hugely insightful into City Hall's confidences and their coffers! Particularly and sententiously when mother & daughter 'philanthropists' Bliss & Lillian are at the helm!

A bush-league farmer in Southern Ontario can get high on how he smells. At best it can be a thankless, remote and solitary existence. The days are long, lengthy long; lonesome and grubby; each humdrum Monday till Monday just held together by blistering sun, choking dust and piercing windswept sleet storms; the reward is cheap.

For an unmarried man life goes slow without love - it moves along inanely, unhurried, the sun rises the sun goes down.

For the married man, he is supposed to spend irrespective interludes in closeness; or so he tells himself. However, it's a long way from the morning to the evening.

In Bliss' existential judgment, if the nett objective is to save souls in bunches then lots of credible cognizance must be given by Anville's plain - spoken and tough-minded public officials. Undoubtedly they had influence to fortify her resolve. Although there were many hyper-critical sensitive arguments over Bliss's 'lollapalooza' cabins at the rear of the Limberlost and maybe some damned good reasons to raise hell about their function; prudence and common sense was inclined to carry the day in the end. Not even one man jack of those crabby city fathers cared to cock a snook of opposition at a discreet 'freebie' as and when required! The Limberlost cabins were indubitably one bald spot that they unanimously choose to ignore!

Bliss' 'Lollapalooza' cabins

CHAPTER NINE

"Mademoiselle from Armentieres parely-voo"

Bliss didn't just want handsome 'working' gals who were seldom good for nothin' else except their looks and their horizontality. Sure, she wanted girls who were not physically repulsive, but moreover she sought out girls who were of 'satisfactory 'size'; girls who were in fine fettle and kind of well fortified. Bliss referred to them as 'gristly' girls who were not amiss to handling a demanding days grind and some cussing too, if it alleviated the days burden for them. She wanted plain stitching, wood splitting, bread yeasting girls and more significantly she didn't want pie in the sky females who were waiting to marry a nonsensical knight errant - or more especially a random Polish troubadour!

Bliss was philosophical about her new venture and chewed over to herself how peculiar it all was; the toing and froing of all those perfidious spouses. Straight-faced and somewhat astonished, she contended that the one unique characteristic about those men who have a taste for wallowing in a cesspool, is that they cannot be made much dirtier by doing it!

With the advent of World War II and Anville having a military establishment close by, Bliss deemed it necessary to arrange regular visits from Anville's Social Protection Officer Betty Andersen. Withal Bliss was highly regarded for the virtuous quality of her girls and she didn't digest the thought of venereal disease and such disrupting her cash crop.

In any event 10 joyful years of fuddled fornication, just justifiably scampered by so quickly, and for et al and Bliss it was 10 most effectual and beneficial years indeed.

But everything runs its course and one day God, out of the blue, realised just how much Bliss loved her fellow man and kindly asked if she would team up with him. I guess he wanted to give the other side of heaven a taster of Bliss' hospitality! I can picture her there right now: wearing silver-coated underwear beneath her cotton twill jeans!

As the afternoon gives up the sun
the shadows lengthened one by one
when God invited Bliss to dance
to give the other side a chance.
How those Sunday bells rang out loud
big men in suits were singing proud

The mind is such an uncannily queer junkyard. It remembers the names of candy bars but cannot remember the Gettysburg Address. It remembers Frank Sinatra's middle name but cannot recall the day a best friend died.

However, in my addled mind there is no such dark corner that does not remember exactly and exclusively the way it happened with Bliss: when George Herman 'Babe' Ruth died and when Bliss Carmen (nee Provenzano).... She just finally ran out of Dixie cups!

CHAPTER TEN

Testa Di Lana!

'And even as I marvelled how
God gives us Heaven here & now
In a stir of wind that hardly shook
The popular leaves beside the brook -
His hand was light upon my brow.'

    From 'Vestigia'

Lillian had always lead an androgynous and individualistic type of life, probably up until Bliss finally met her maker during the Indian summer of '49. As far as relationships were concerned the local farm boys were pretty gauche, and she wasn't really struck on being 'sequestrated' by some roughshod hick in the back of his pa's barn. And as for Saturday night dances; most could easily be likened to hormone day at a mink ranch!

The girls of her age were inclined to be sorrowfully soppy. They were either riding their cotton bicycle of domestic affliction or otherwise infelicitously interbreeding like professional blind dates.

"Love will come one day" she thought. "Maybe just at the last moment., Like in the movies". Lillian just had to believe that hokey sentiment, or else there just wasn't any reason for her to be merely eighteen.

Although Lillian embraced a certain kind of schmaltzyness in her outlook upon a persons partiality to loving; she nevertheless was minded more toward incontrovertible questions (and assertions) rather than any old and outdistanced platitudes. What's more she was invariably more that a ski jump ahead of her would-be cynics, if only (but not entirely) in her gee-whiz bonhomie wonderment of the planet in general. Lillian also seemed to have an almost congenital disposition toward Mother Nature: plants, animals and such. She loved to keep and eye on the lazy longhorns as they fettled in the ample pasture on yonder side of Winter Creek. She like how they scratched their behinds on the barnyard doors and switched their tails at the irritating flying insects: and their gamy dialogue as they chewed their endless cuds.

Sometimes Lillian would walk up the hill to the meadow, just to get the longhorns perspective on what <u>she</u> looked like, sitting on the further side of Winter Creek. She once told them: "the young can save the world by growing older and wiser like you - we need men and women with truths and brand new dignity like yours" - and then she tempestuously went home. Always looking, always seeking, always needing something more - that was Lillian Carmen.

But change is change, it's unaccountable, yet in spite of that it's always surprising when it comes to call on you - seemingly without justification - or hiking down <u>your</u> highway to <u>your</u> home.

Lillian wasn't that fond of change in any of its divergent disguises. Even in her choice of books , when all is said and done she preferred to read a novel whose story she was familiar with. Rather than a story by some highfalutin neurotic writer whom she had not yet tried and tested.

When she was a sophomore, Lillian had pleasingly become acquainted with Jane Austen. Although she had read and enjoyed her novels many times, Lillian especially savoured Jane's realistic attitude to all the goings-on. Much like her own life, Jane's world may have been a microcosm of sort but how well she knew it. Chawton in Hampshire was an exceedingly far-flung mise en scéne however, here on the grassy banks of Winter Creek Lillian's world and Jane's world were about to be somewhat refreshingly aired.

The wide-branched trees stood as if they were paralyzed in the windless air, their leafy tops so dusty green and cicada filled. For Lillian alone there was something quite wicked, forbidden and excitingly peculiar about the unique environment of Winter Creek that particular spring evening.

Bliss however, had a completely different modus operandi in mind. She knew that all of her dandelion days were done and that she wasn't likely to receive any more wild promises from any young men, but nonetheless, she had a craving to be one of those avant-garde females that the newspapers were persistently ballyhooing over. Except for Shirley Temple and Orphan Annie every woman around in those post-war prosperity days - on television, in films, in ads and even in the humour of the day - were constructed to either discuss, joke about or deeply analyze how to be attractive and consummately expert with their sexual impulses and slushy mushy notions.

Prior to WWII the essence of any sexual matter would best be 'avoided' by reading "self and sex" by William Briggs (1897). This series (which was only distributed for Canadian readers) could fairly be procured by way of a variety of established drug stores. It was about as hot as pleasurable as an ice cream in a blizzard!

In any event bliss had become a recurrent traveller on the first and last bus to Hamilton every second Wednesday. Somewhat twitchy, looking like the cat's whiskers and preparing herself for a pampering, this was her day! A little waxing, a little electrolysis, a mani/pedicure; senility has its privileges! Amidst the infirmities of age, it was a comfort to Bliss, that, whatever destruction time worked on her memory, she never found it affecting her judgment. Needless to say, 'La Belle Femme' was a complementarity to all septuagenarians!

And so for an interim period at least Lillian had become the titulor head honcho of Limberlost; although to tell the truth she was ever so wistful of an uninterrupted and peaceful evening. Wednesdays were normally quiet - or so she thought!

She knew by the smoke that so peacefully curled
Above the green elms, that there was nothing to fear;
And she said, if there's peace to be found in the world
A heart that is humble might hope for it here.

It wasn't that long before she heard a vehicle park-up on the forecourt and heavy set footsteps stomping in her direction across the lawn. It must have been shortly after six o'clock that Nicolai Dostolevsky turned up at the Limberlost. Lillian had no indication that he was due to call on them that evening and she was kind of vexed that Bliss had done nothing to rein back his visit - until <u>she</u> was here to deal with it.

43

Lillian savoured her Cinderellaly solitary moments when Bliss was away on business and such; they were important to her. In fact it was as though she took on a new and detached type of identity; perhaps it came with responsibility. However, one thing was for sure, there was nothardly any telling whatsoever of her inclinations or intentions. It was as though she had just graduated from the Copacabana school of acting and was out to make a distinguishable impression on life. Her jesting and her seriousness were so intertwined that the actual message she was sending was open to the speculativeness of the individual. One thing was for sure though, she was able to inveigle literally anyone at all, and moreover she was totally unerring in her instincts of spotting pretension and phoniness a mile away.

In all seriousness Lillian was much more that just a face-lift of dissimilarity away from Bliss. For example, laying hidden in Bliss was a chest load of sorrow and emptiness that remained untenanted long after she had passed on into the next world. I remember how strange I thought it was when in later years Lillian opened-up and told me how she never considered herself to be Bliss's 'proper' bastard. Said it was because she could never imagine Bliss being capable of any sort of act of sexual immorality.

I guess that whilst times have changed some and morals with them; in 1913 it must really have been considered immoral indeed to mother a child without being married. I only wish that times had changed the sooner, rather than the later - if only to have kept Bliss from feeling guilty; if indeed she ever did!

Lillian crossed her legs in a seemly lady-like fashion. Her vulgar check list of Nicolai Dostolevsky was coming up trumps - he did look like a cheap hood, but credit where it's due, because at the same time he had a great talent for gettin' away with his wickedness as well.

Lillian began to speak to him as though she were explaining a troublesome problem in algebra to an imbecile who had no inclination or notion whatsoever towards mathematics. Barber shop banter was more his taste.

Come to think of it, I guess that Nicolai was somewhat taken about by Lillian's snarky and contemptuous stance toward his so-called

44

dispensation of matters. He was caught by the balls, somewhere between exasperated and disbelief - an awful vulnerable place to be!

Lillian had a pet raccoon once who stole her toothbrush. However, she forgave him because he was 'so cute'. Unequivocally, there was not an iota of adorability regarding this of late heister.

She had heard about his scuzzy methods of doing business and his infamous ambitions to truss up local restaurateurs under his auspices. Invading their turf didn't sit well with the bosses of the other clans also - who, in any event had Limberlost under <u>their</u> own umbrella, - and for sure it didn't sit well with Lillian either! In accordance with what is morally right, Lillian figured that Nicolai Dostolevsky's reckless assumptions on the health of her elderly mother were an affront. To attempt to shake down the infirmed was improper and inexcusable and downright disrespectful!

There was a pause - they were all waiting: the cicada filled trees for rain, Nicolai Dostolevsky for his just desserts and Lillian for her moment...

She stood up suddenly; violently; aloofly. Unexpectedly the expression across her face changed; it became soft, almost sympathetic - her eyes smoky in colour. "My strong, wicked darling" she uttered as she blew the white carnation in his button hole to little-bitty smithereens with just one .45 bullet.

Dostolevsky was dead so fast that his Havana cigar was still smoking in his mouth as Lillian gratuitously rolled him down the embankment of Winter Creek and into the consolatory lukewarm waters.

It was the same old story of Dostolevsky's gluttonous life - he was a freelance, a manipulator who liked to have his grubby hands in everyone's pie; but once too often!

If he had listened hard enough he might have heard what Lillian meant to say...Nothing! My own estimation is that he had endeavoured to collect an interest that was not rightly his to collect and Lillian had rightly handed him a delinquent one-way ticket to Polookaville.

I think that Dostolevsky was one of those hoods who never really cared to know the answers. There are still some who want to know, who dare to try to know, but Dostolevsky was not one of them. That's why no one saw, no one cared to notice and no one could possibly say what had occurred that unimportant Wednesday evening. Bliss though commendably observed that there hadn't been such a dandified corpse as Nicolai's in Winter Creek since before 1920!

Winter Creek – Late Spring

Winter Creek – December

CHAPTER ELEVEN

Unelaborated truths

When we're eating popcorn at the movies and you smile at me and not the pictures; I kind of know that I am not wrong - about us!

<u>Jacques Leyrac circa 1961</u>

The Montreal Gazette December 18/1959...

...The sweet smell of instant success came for newcomer Kim Denisa last night. This 20 year old European soprano received an exceptionally rapturous reception after she thoroughly captivated the first audiences at Theatre Saint-Denis. Miss Denisa is the daughter of an Anglo Polish mother and spent the war years in Nazi-occupied Poland (often in near starvation!)

Mother and daughter immigrated to Canada during 1945 and were reunited with Kim's Polish/Canadian father.

Kim is indeed a rare phenomenon and an original in every respect: Such a chiffony gamine in appearance and yet she carriers herself with an ethereal and dauntess grace. Her entrance on stage showed an almost innate sense of theatricality and radiance, unsurpassed in someone so young.

There was such an almighty hubbub of a gathering outside of her dressing room throughout the brief twenty minute or so interval.

Quite meticulously and unreservedly she acknowledged every admirer as though they all were her most intimate companions. Pressing her way forward through all of the shimmering evening gowns and sharp dinner jackets and finally pausing central to their gaze. She walked, talked, stood and smiled every inch the confident elegant diva, yet in the depthless chasms of her disguised opinions she pained like an undiscovered child at it wits end. By some chance perhaps that was why she was able to smile at folks in such a wry way that it would right away revive the secret self in <u>them</u> - or at the very least it would improve their perception of life. Though 'tis a pity it didn't somehow do the same for her.

In spite of, or perhaps because of, Kim's rather tenuous grasp of reality it did her good to spend time with Jacques. They enjoyed many loquacious evenings together at Jacques' Montreal apartment in that, their first winter.

Almost intuitively Kim was becoming aware that somewhere out there in Jacques' high-toned yet isolated past he had suffered equally as she indeed had. The tragedy was that despite all of their rather uncanny comparability, neither of them felt so inclined to 'open up' or dwell upon it; and so therefore, they still suffered alone.
However, they had plenty of laughs and what was more they shared such an amazing requited connection that could not bear comparison or equivalence of any kind.

Throughout all of those 'hysterical' days of Kim finally 'coming of age' Jacques was to become so much more than purely Kim's musical mentor. He taught her almost everything: how to dress, how to comport 'oneself' and... How to bake bread! Not just any old plain bread making recipes, but how to prepare and bake loaves the Le Parrain way - the way in which Jacques was instructed when he lived with his friend years ago.

Several days on from Jacques 'specialized' coaching there was an unexpected knock on his apartment door.

Deeply demure, Kim had arrived with three 12 inch loaves - still warm and in their tins - that she had meticulously baked!

Jacques remarked: (somewhat incredulously) "smells good Kim". "Smells restful Jacques" she replied sedately.

Jacques had pondered on how she could imagine that the bread smelt 'restful'. But you know she was right, he thought; it did!

"Strombol Bread - but without the capicola"; she stressed. "Just like your friend used to make Jacques".

It was around early daybreak when Jacques hinted about calling Kim a cab. They had spent the evening tinkering around the piano keys. Everything was on offer from Brubeck to Offenback and Kim sang a little too.

As Jacques said goodnight to her in the lobby, Kim reflected: "Do you realize Jacques that women are concave and men are convex?" "How do you work that one out?" Jacques replied. Kim just smiled and planted a kiss on Jacques' cheek "Well aren't we?" she enquiringly replied.

Knowing Jacques he probably would have agreed with her and smiled right back - far better than any smile that she'd ever known. If he had decided to emphasize a frown, it would have been the sort of comical frown that you can only share with a special friend!

The times they had, the times that cannot ever be bought with nickels & dimes. At times like these she would often respond with teasing supplementaries, such as referring to Jacques as her 'George Du Maurier' [1]. Jacques never figured out the meaningfulness of it; viz 'George Du Maurier'... But I had a hunch or two that I kept suppressed!

Jacques and Kim just fitted together like a productive whole - perhaps it was on the requite and somewhat loquacious understanding by them both that two tipsy people functioning together is far happier arrangement than one so-called free soul alone. In any event neither of them had been able to push the clouds away by themselves and so being on the opposite side of harmony would have been an opportunity missed indeed!

Every generation gap should have some kind of bridge, even if it's only made of love. However, the question that is most pertinent remains unanswered: are they both ready for it? Or are there vital aspects that they need to address in the privacy of reflection. Jacques knows about life, love and compromise but although he has lived his life alone for many years, has he really been lonely? Kim on the other hand has only ever known the authoritative nature that seems to be prevalent in many men - inasmuch that

---

[1] French-born author of the novel 'Trilby'. The story of a natural singer able to perform only under the hypnosis of Svengali, her tutor.

they should be obeyed without question! - as with her father Renek. Could it be that for Kim to see herself as a new functioning whole person, without a man to prop her up, may be a somewhat difficult identity to embrace at this very speculative stage-managed phase in her life.

Someday the world they know may come along and bid them to go because sometimes life has a proneness to interfere in things not entirely of our making. Spring may chase them through the Summer and into fall until slowly, slowly the creative puzzle that is their existence will kick-start and suddenly it will be spring again for them, that's the way I see it!

Be that as it may, it is slightly unlikely to occur until all of the shifting shapes of destiny have been allowed leeway to rise and fall on numerous times for them, and that's a pity. Even now at this stage they have both learned so much. Perhaps everything that they need to learn has already been learnt...apart from how to stay in touch!

Now soon, ah, soon I know
The trumpets of the North will blow,
And the great winds will come to bring
The pale wild riders of the snow.

BLISS CARMEN, "Before the snow", 1916

The Ontario snow was tinkling much faster than either Kim or Jacques imagined that it would, during this their first winter together - it invariably was so, so capricious; that powered Ontario snow.

No mortal soul could ever suppose or assume the profound happy-go-luckyness of schleping with all of their deliberation through endless gardens of generously bountiful Ontario snow.

Snow is a metaphor for everything, but above all else it is symbolic of love. It can provide all of what you desire and it will pledge to ensure that all of your sought-after dreams and desires are safe and flying free.

Unless it missed attention; snow is simply, 'unelaborated'.

CHAPTER TWELVE

"Mama canned peaches"

Life should have a game plan
But it doesn't.,
A 'need' should know exactly where it's going
- but it seldom does

Leroy Stooduhs lived in a log cabin at the edge of town that amounted to little more than a grocery store and several workaday houses. Nevertheless, it still qualified for a name: STRONGARM' - down a road, north of Thunder Bay!

From first appearances the cabin looked comparatively primitive - like it might have been built by Lincoln (or out of Lincoln logs!). However, inside the cabin was a wonderment to behold: it was spacious, comfortable and modern.

Attached to the main building by a covered walkway was an annex, which nicely served as Leroy's gymnasium, sauna and his self-styled Church of Christendom. All the walls were mirrored floor to ceiling in burnt umber tint, except for an alcove which contained a large framed picture of the crucifixion. There seemed to be freshly cut flowers in glass vases on every flat surface throughout. If I had any predispositions toward exaggeration I would not even buy one red ribbon to furnish that room further!

Dear Krystyna/Kim

If you mother's womb had a view
You would never have ventured out!

When God gave her Jacques it was because she had prayed with caution and when Jacques gave her a safe place she became surrounded by the self-assurance he put up for her. For today and tomorrow she could see beyond the wall that one-time was beyond <u>that</u> wall. She felt competent to take any outstretched hand and offer her own outstretched hand to anyone who smiled at her from out of a multi-coloured window.

Wearing mascara on her eyelashes, a Garbo hat and a $800 dress that looked like it belonged to Ann Landers - they were the lesser undoings of sorts - the more serious undoings genuinely escaped her notice that awful Wednesday afternoon.

It took her better part of the day to reach 'Strongarm' but by the time she'd parked up she was smiling like a convent cat in the knowledge that she's driven there all on her own.

She crossed the street to Leroy's recognizable cabin and couldn't stop presuming that every house window held a pair of eyes that stared out and unmasked her silent betrayal of safe places and Jacques Leyrac.

She half expected that Spanish dancers would come bursting through the doors, vests and petticoats of every colour, heels stomping, snapping, clicking ready for some fine fiesta. Such was the conceptualized vividness of Leroy's anecdotal storylines and uniquely his preoccupation and total enthusiasm over everything Spanish - from the Inquisition to his Spanish shoe maker, Leroy Strooduhs and Spain belonged to one another.

Mackenzie King's attitude during the Spanish Civil War reflected the sympathy of many Catholic Quebecers for Franco - Leroy's own naiveté after his father was shot during the Iberian dust-up never found solace for him. Unless all the yatter regarding Spain was his alleviation from it.

After dining upon Leroy's entertainingly tall talkativeness, Kim amused herself by just gaming around the gymnasium. Leroy told her he had no objections, provided she say a prayer for her restitution at bedtime! She gazed at herself in the mirrors; methodically pedalling the exercise bicycle and was dead set that she wouldn't be returning to Jacques Leyrac - she was sick of being his so-called 'whiz-kid'. And she was too pleased, excited and impressed to have just pulled up stakes and left Jacques. In her disillusioned judgment she surmised that Jacques had 'disillusioned' her in any event!

Kim was around 20 years of age when she first ran into Leroy Stooduhs. She was insociant and vulnerable and was at once mesmerized by the debonair and charming, blond-haired, blue-eyed theatrical broker.

What actually happened was; during the intermission between first and second showing of Premingers 'Exodus' Jacques was scheduled to present Mrs John Diefenbaker. It was opening night of the movie and Jacques had tried for months to get the Diefenbakers to attend - finally Mrs Diefenbaker had agreed. Jacques was a big fan of theirs: "first darned Prime Minister of this country of neither English nor French origin" he was very emotive about them!

Kim was twiddling her thumbs playing a slower than usual game of solitaire in Jacques' Toronto place of work - awaiting his return. Her advanced stage of boredom and restlessness, factored into 40 minutes of ostentatiousness, was to altogether reshape her life. Leroy Strooduhs had unwittingly made just a customary drop in on Jacques in order to acquire a band singer and instead he got his hands on a tailor-made 'acolyte'.

It was ten to one the most understated short shrift when Jacques subsequently told Kim that she was liable to throw away what was beginning to be a glorious career - to become a band singer! No doubt Jacques was in awe of the reverberations that may follow, and although he was full and filled with firm conviction, sometimes courage comes in short supply - each of us can only work at it and try!

She followed Leroy to the netherworld that he inhabited, that lies just beyond the trees. Where the grass is emerald green and where every person lives to at least a hundred and twenty four.

It wasn't entirely her responsibility in any event, Jacques had his contribution - or so she reasoned!

But she was more experienced now and Leroy Strooduhs or whatshisname are all pretty repossessing when you are muddled and a massive boredom tiptoes in. Maybe Leroy wasn't such a deleterious character after all, considering that (unbeknownst to him) he did die for her! And Kim is also worthy of praise or respect because she did do her ultimate duty and attend Leroy's funeral.

Apparently, it was an exceptionally raw day when they laid Leroy to rest - even the gravediggers were behind schedule because the ground was so frozen. Kim told me that as the snow and ice crunched under her shoes she felt unimaginably warm. It was as though he was cuddled up under her cloths in all of his nefarious splendour. She said that she was impervious to the ceremony and all that she recalled was the amusing yarns he would tell her at supper time.

In the early days after Leroy gave up his job sellin' shoes to become a so-called impresario, his bills at that time were picked up by an older than him lady named Ruth Pickering. Ruth thought that he was a bright young man and began chasin' him for a bit of here and there love.

When I was starting up the hill, I too thought that Leroy might be able to crack the whip on my fledgling career. That was until his blood alcohol level registered above .08 per cent. The last time I saw Leroy was outside of Loblaws in Stoney Creek - a cop was waving traffic past. No ambulance had yet arrived but two police cars were keeping guard on the Coroner's new dibs. I slowed but I didn't stop, withal what good was a manager going to be if he was dependent upon a Greyhound Bus- about as useless as evolution in reverse, I guess.

However, in view of Leroy's recent demise and in the event that I were to dash off a homily to him, this would be my attempt to elucidate the misconceptions regarding the late Leroy Strooduhs, as follows:

Leroy really loved his mother; his eyes would often fill with tears when he talked about her. "Mama canned peaches and currants and washed our cloths in the bath tub by hand" he enthused. "I just love to open my eyes at night and see her sitting at the foot of the bed inviting me to join her in God's wonderful world. He went on to explain that although his mother had taught him all the things a man must never forget, she had neglected to teach him how to die!" "I want to make sure I do it correctly" he would say excitedly, "but I don't know how!". Kim was kind of stunned at this self-judgment that Leroy had about death.

Kim said that he once asked her if she thought death would be like slipping on a wet sidewalk but not awakening after you hit the concrete! She said that the image was just so ludicrous and so asinine to her and paled all of her would-be metaphysical answers in comparison.

Leroy also mentioned that he didn't believe in the concept of heaven and hell, he figured that they both are with us right here and now!

It seems to me that the somewhat misguided Mr Strooduhs had some kind of resident death wish that required gratification. In which case he was most probably relieved (in a philosophical sense) when it eventually crossed his path.

I guess that one of the fundamental principles in Leroy's life was the almost divine certainty of his resolutions. And with that in mind his conscious decision to abide by his mother's wishes were not so outlandish; in spite of suggestions otherwise.

The clergy who drum into their congregations, litanies that have no relevance with common speech have lost the plot; and so how can Leroy ever be trespassing in an idealistic utopia which his (unlikely) logic has fervently sacrificed into existence?

CHAPTER THIRTEEN

The Iroquoian experience

Thar's good & bad in Injun,
An' thar's good & bad in white;
But, somehow, they is allus wrong,
An' we is allus right!

Grandpa John E. Logan (1915)

Canada's war on the Indians was not a shooting war like it had been in the U.S. It was purely a long war of attrition and is still being waged to this day. It inflicts new defeats on every new generation and the horrifying weapon we use is indifference.

These first Americans have their own incomparable way of life as well as their own gracious way of death. Their attitude toward death is entirely consistent with their unique character and their elegant philosophy. Death has no terrors for them and they meet death with a philosophical and a moral simplicity, seeking only an honourable end as a last gift of remembrance to their family and their descendants. Intrepidly they may court death in battle, however, they would regard death as disgraceful (perhaps wasteful) to be killed in a private or futile quarrel, as we tend to do.

In this chapter I discovered that the 'afterwash' was far more difficult to explain (let alone comprehend) than I imagined it would be: in any event perhaps it is not my prerogative to try to do so.

And so as a starting place of sorts I have adhered purely to the evidence/facts and respectfully allowed my reader to make their own inferences.

In this instance it was the only process of ever reaching a satisfactory conclusion I could think of.

Their appalling story is long and continuing, but fortunately for me, mine isn't. In any event I couldn't write their story, I am neither qualified or unsqeamish enough to attempt such a venture. You see, I too, fall into the 'white' convenience of double negatives that categorizes all first Americans as 'Indians'. In actuality they originally consisted of over 500 different nations, comprised of simply millions of individuals: alas no more!

It is only because this isolated account of their sharp-wittedness and graciousness intertwines with "Limberlost" that I have endeavoured to give light to just a handful of these depleted first Americans

Somewhere where the stars are all strung together and are stringing out infinite across the vault of heaven; and where the moon hangs half hung against the raw indigo sky; and where the burnt sienna landscape lies-down and mourns for spring - somewhere huddles the little-bitty village called Onondaga.

Onondaga lies kind of due South of the Great Lakes, however, without the benefit of a military reconnoitre, I definitely could not go back and find it again.

I am not that sure that I ever really knew exactly the location of Onondaga, however, chance and sheer luck were good travelling buddies in those heady days and I think I may have lost them en route.

I suppose it was one of those self-righteous occasions when I believed that I was helping to open a stuck door for an old friend, but whilst I briefly looked the other way he unintentionally shut the door on my fingers. My own fault, I should have kept a closer watch!

Over ferns, nettles and through swarms of mosquitoes thirsting for blood we traversed. Him, whistling and singing sweet Sunday psalms out clear and strong; every word and warble coming up from his immense chest with meaningful resolve and vigour. In later life I wondered who we both became, out there in the underbrush. He indubitably was Errol Flynn. Me, I kind of felt like the Scarlet Pimpernel, on a mission! I guess that whatever new persona a person decides to adopt, it's almost certain to be someone famous and fabulous - and slightly villainous! Indeed to be someone that wasn't there before. The rescue of cats and dogs and infant children, just have that over melodramatic effect on us poor mortals.

I spoke on the telephone with him just twelve hours ago regarding the whereabouts of his child: I knew a has-been drum majorette with a metaphorical batteried baton; she knew all the whispers for a fifty mile radius!

"I'll pack a bag for Canada straight away" he impassively replied.

I could just picture him on the other end of the telephone: bold ass collecting streaks, sat there on his uncomfortable bamboo davenport; gracefully reaching for his Spencer carbine and raising it to his eye...yes, that would be the customary course of events!

It seemed to me that he never did like living in Canada that much, and had a greater liking for the other side of the border - at least that was the impression I got. Said to me that he wouldn't recommend living in Canada as a way of life. However, he inoffensively added "who is going to say which side is better or worse, till they've been there and found what they are searching for?" The way that I interpreted that comment was that there was no wrong or right side of the border - things are not necessarily more dependable in either Michigan or Ontario; and the fields are beginning to have the selfsame empty colour this time of the year in any event.

McAffee's hardware store was always more crowded during the winter months, inasmuch that the local farmers were hard pressed for a moment of rest during the summer months - McAffee;s kind of became a place to meet and meddle when temperatures fell below zero.

This particular day it was nary a fit day for a fence post and the majority of them had stockpiled a mess of loquaciousness, cooped-up all summer long. Several hours around the range at McAffee's was an exemplary way to shoot the breeze and although all of their supposings and composings mattered little and solved nothing; it was an excellent way of frustrating and exasperating a headache where a pill can't reach!

Following the burning summer of '62 the onset of winter was certainly threatening to be equally as uncompromising. That said a small party of Indians had decided to 'winter' on the sheltered flank of Winter Creek: It offered some protection due to the proximity of woodland.

However, the sudden disappearance of Joey McCracken's Alsatian was sufficient to start a hue and cry like a gaggle of priest dispensing holy water: "Sonsofbitches all of em., they'd eat a dead skunk through a screen door with a toothpick". There were all the usual expletives generally kept in reserve for such an occasion - including some I hadn't come across previously. Strange how the angle of the loon's leg always gets a blast!

Now, there are those of us who suffer blindness when faced by an exceptional sunset and there are those of us whose eyes take on a keener field of vision purely by the amounts of carrots they consume - and then unfortunately, there are those of us who prefer to remain blissfully blinkered. I guess whatever empty tree a person lives in, the wind will still tremble through it, it cannot be ignored out of ignorance, can it?

Americas first inhabitants were also the last inhabitants who were entirely democrative and enshrouded free spirits in human form. However, time has done very little to diminish the impulsiveness of us whites, and it wouldn't have mattered one iota to us that Joey McCracken's Alsatian dog was killed when it was sideswiped by an enormous truck outside of the Limberlost; the driver never even heard the bump but fate 'believed' the reverberation; it really wanted to!

Perhaps in essence we are kind of like those first Americans after all. But unlike them we have somehow lost all of our valuable 'shamans'. Therefore, the only positive; nay effective way we can deal with common yet important issues is to participate in some kind of group psychotherapy; circa a hardware store range. The farmers never failed from any lack of exerting themselves, that was for sure!

Spirit of the air,

Come down,

Come down!

Your shaman calls

<u>INUIT SONG</u>

Finally the wind stopped piling up the November leaves and turned to drive the snow in drifts along the fences. And finally the white clouds were overtaking the grey clouds and the day began to slip in.

At six o'clock in the morning it never rained on any corner of Limberlost acreage - it just never did! It was as though the elements of nature had completed their night time stint and everything around had paused for just an interim period before the day shift was to take over.

Mom understood about anomalous happenings - not especially relating to birds and butterflies and such, but to a greater extent she understood the significance and needfulness of canoes and coffee and pots & pans and bickering.

And so she took a pail of tetchy water and sterilizer and expeditiously swished the animals blood & innards off the lonesome highway.

Alas the poor pitiful dog was not that much cumbersome to carry "he was just all ribs and ticks" Mom said dourly. However, just before the 7:30am breakfast rush he was jollying along to becoming Cannelloni filling, allied with an appropriate apportion of Bechamel sauce and garlic.

He was like a gypsy vagabond that dog. He'd walked all the roads around Anville and played across every meadow and hill. He had almost become part of the landscape himself, and so perhaps it was not that inharmonious of Mom to decide to 'mementorize' the hapless creature for futurity like she did. Now only the summer vacationers who enjoyed eating outdoors in the picnic grounds still used the mossy old outside John, and this time of the year not even the flies were interested. And so appropriately that was where Mom agreed it would be a perfect location to staple his hide - thereabouts to the outer door and its lintel, for the purposes of 'preserving and curing'. Just after Christmas when all the curing had been accomplished, Mom pruned off the scraggly ends and utilized the fur skin as a lap robe in her precious old Ford Roadster. It always kind of cheered Mom up when folks remarked how neat and novel the lap robe was. Mom was an inventive and thrifty lady, she was not at all one of those modernity throw-away types!

A mardi gras of expletives run riot in my head when deliberating over the delicacy of the word 'virtue'; and its meaning. Curiously, it seems to me that we may have arrived at a place and a time where the fine old original meaning of 'virtue' is actually no longer to be considered as a virtue per se. Perhaps virtue has unwittingly permitted itself to become a kind of personable cliché of the twentieth century, because as often as not it has become fairly riddled with self-centered libertinism of late.

The seismic mention of the word 'virtue' used to be very selective and would invariably only be utilized to denote an important enactment or to nominate a significant person or occasion: where all provisos have been taken into account.

Peculiar through it seems, the definition of 'virtue' has become alien to us, it is no longer a wonderfully intimate portrait to savour and enjoy - and that, I feel is so noxiously off balance!

In any event whatever wish-book of dynamic forethought we care to rummage through; it would be extremely difficult to imagine how a sixteen year old single parent could immerse herself in purposeful determination to set things right. Two jobs, a son in kindergarten and yet she still had money left for discoveries at the Salvation Army thrift store. It was important for her that she and her son wear respectable cloths.

She tried to act and behave like a woman but beneath her facade of bravery she walked, talked and smiled like a little girl.

Mercifully the bars and clubs were often dark enough so as she wouldn't be recognized as a minor, however, Sarah Smith was also an Indian and that was her unfortunate giveaway.

She and her son lived in an apartment just off Main Street West in Hamilton. It was at basement level so that most of the time it was dark inside, and the only view of the street was of peoples' feet: going back and forth across the windows. Once in a while a man's footsteps would pause, a faceless man with sandpaper hands and black impersonal nails: breathing like a shadow in total delirium of communication: and then melting away across the windows once more.

With body humiliated, with nerves stretched (the soul doesn't even get a look in) another day in the slowest form of non-existence is over. It's true that from time to time every little sparrow may come home alone and forgotten about by the sun and rain of surviving - but why so inequitably unbalanced is life?

It was early in the a.m. When they arrested Sarah Smith; on the corner of Elizabeth and Dundas. She had been on the streets for twelve hours flat and felt so dazed and confused that she couldn't even answer to her name. She wasn't really sure where they were taking her, whether she wanted to go or what she intended to do; but she realized her son needed to get away from this life and from her, and that she had to get away from herself.

Sarah Smith was sentenced to eighty days corrective work on the Honor Farm in a relatively rural area, about forty miles north of Sainte-Marie. Although the days on the farm were somewhat long and wearing, there was something intangible yet very consolable to be gained from them: she arose at 5:30 am precisely, ate an adequate breakfast and began her assignments with milking the facilities' cows until around 7:30 am. All of the girls spent the remainder of their day on the land: planting and picking. The evenings were comparatively noiseless. For many of the girls, like Sarah, this was their first incarceration and so killing off the need to be set loose was not so effortless as they had envisaged.

It was during such a mid-week evening that Sarah Smith chose to compose her swan song to Bob.

Bob Mitcham was a Methodist lay minister by trade, he leased a small-holding in Michigan; he was also the father of Sarah Smith's child. Bob was despised by the Iroquoi, who consequential to Sarah Smith's arrest the child was now living with.

All of the room in Sarah's correspondence to Bob was taken up by her pipe dreams. He had invaded her little world with his virtuousness and now he was indelible upon her heart. She smiled as she carefully drew the x's at the ending of her letter. In those fields of wonder there were no overhead steam pipes, no peeling walls, no disinfectant smelling dark corners; solely her and Bob. Beyond hello and before the obligatory good-bye there were also a string of words that a person could get killed for, two paragraphs that a person could probably have been killed for, and an exceptionally uneasy ending - but that wouldn't worry Bob; would it?

Early on the morning of the twenty-third I wakened with a start; someone was frying ham & eggs in my kitchen! Before I had properly opened my eyes, I guessed what was going on. Bob had bumped the door lock and let himself in - "didn't want to wake you" he considerately said! It always gave me a chuckle how Bob could come into your home and make himself at home; so quickly! He was stood there in his long johns and woollen socks; his boots, pants and topcoat steaming for all they were worth on the stove overhang. My bony old mouser seemed to enjoy the stifling pong of Bob's cloths and the frizzling food and had arched its back and was rubbing mournfully against Bob's leg.

I have known Bob for many years and indeed I am grateful for it. He'd take his own outstretched hand and offer it to any pilgrim who was in need. To be sure he taught me that my hour in heaven would be guaranteed if I were to do the same.

Bob was invariably far more than a regular buddy. Moreover, he was a special breed of compatriot who not only made you question what he was doing here with you, but also made you sanely query what you were doing here with him!

We made our way up the Devil's Pathway to Onondaga - it was a fairly rugged stretch of byroad that mostly ran parallel to the shoreline. Bob was all for taking an alternative route cross-country no matter how bucolic it was. It was as though he had an unconscious desire to ignite his penned up emotions and getting to Onondaga quicker would put it all right. I was beginning to have some serious misgivings regarding the underlying purpose of our journey. It was one of these situations where it's too late to get off the roundabout, but in all honesty I was wishing that I were home - wherever that may be - or that I'd left some of my misgivings at home!

So anyways, we'd been stepping on it down this rural back road for perhaps some eighty miles; the tall grass was twisting in the dusk breeze, I was enjoying one of Bob's Lucky's and my mind was beginning to feel settled again - until hot vapour began to throw itself all over the windshield; and that was that!

It seems to me that there are some outlandish occasions when a person should stop and count their blessings; no matter of the circumstances at hand. Although our vehicle had now become something of a problem, to every other extent it was the most beautiful and picturesque evening imaginably.

The backdrop of the sunset had kind of blurred itself into such an amazing mass of single pastel colour, set against Bob's 'still' steaming red Pontiac. It put me in mind of Mom's chunky china stacked up and condensating after being steam washed.

Unaccompanied as we were by our divining sticks, it became impossible for us to locate water for the Pontiac's radiator out there in the boondocks.

However, in the event that a similar catastrophe should happen to you, and it might, just be less pessimistic and more systematic and obey my simple directives, as follows:-

1: Take a leisurely drink or two.
2: Relax and rest-up.
3: Listen to the unique accompaniment of the crickets and frogs.
4: Assiduously piss into the rad!

Bob taught me that! And then he turned the Pontiac's nose around and pointed it in the direction of Anville - Bob was determined that we wouldn't be outstaying our welcome once we had the kid in our possession.

Out there in the sticks, a man is nothing more than a tear that has been wiped aside by God. All the vastness of space is taken up by the gullies of an empty belly and the curves and turns it takes to put food on the table. Remembering the people who forgot your name is long past being a main consideration of the tribes.

As we started up the hill, I could smell the rancid smoke from their longhouse - they were burning green sticks I think. As we were drawing nearer to the long house I could hear mutable music - Roger Miller or Willie Nelson I think. As Bob ploughed through the longhouse door, rifle in hand and me by his side; I felt like a seraph gone nutso! So why was I here?

They sat there motionless, maybe 20 or 30 Indians; male, female, children, in vague circles of gauzy smoke.

The shadowed afternoon was moving into evening now, and all that could be visually made out for sure were the hickory branches held tightly and conscientiously by each member of the tribe. Strikingly, the bark had been stripped off each branch and so the exposed wood had a kind of illuminating effect.

The head man just gazed straight through Bob, it was as though he was carefully devouring Bob's entire physiognomy and mindfully substituting it with his own.

A silence like a huge ticking clocking-out book descends into the room as if we were about to be pensioned off. We were so wrongfully amiss to invade their invaluable world in this manner. Self-righteously we assumed that we held the moral high ground, but they had envisaged that in advance. They just waited passively for our ridiculous and uncompromising entrance. They were smarter and slicker than us and we realized it.

It seemed that only at only this precise moment we discovered how to choose - only at this precise moment when we were out of choice of anything we might have been able to choose. Indeed a total voluptuousness regarding absence of any plausible choice was ours in its entirety - implicitly, we were grimly washed up!

I tried to remain calm but I could just hear a slaughter house in my brain. People commenting "what a horridly mutilated body - and such an awful loss of blood!" I thought of the movies I had seen about people during the Second World War, where the unsung heroes life plays out before him in the greatest of detail, in the briefest of moments.

I questioned my sanity for getting myself entangled with all of Bob's connubial catastrophe. I didn't really know that much about it in any event, and I didn't really care much either. However, Bob was my friend and abandoning him when he needed a helping hand was never an option. Anyways, kidnapping a child is almost a major industry in some of those irreverent European countries! And I would have been displeased if Bob had kept his son's whereabouts to himself and gone it alone.

But the question I was asking myself remains; what was I doing out there in the sticks, almost lingering (as the condemned do) between my fruitful life just zooming past me and with the unknowable unknown so iniquitously imminent.

I thought about the taste of Mom's beer (second to none since she decontaminated the metal pipes) and that old Limberlost Wurlitzer (where the 45's remain unchanged) and I thought about my new-fangled exotic best friend Matilda Berceanu (who has a weakness for singing Lascia ch'io Pianga in the nude)

Do not think me sorry for myself, I was not. I had in fact no immortal sense of myself left any longer. But I was desperately going through the motions again; especially as I watched Bob lowering his skirmishing rifle from his squinty eye.

I was unaware that God was such a complicated man and with such a riotous sense of humour to boot; because that especial day God the funky friend and not God the Father came heavenly knocking on Bob's combative door of ridiculousness.

Bob was foundering on the brink of failure with only one ace left up his sleeve. He smiled kind of superfluously at the Chief and made every struggling effort to express his regret, but the Chief was having none of it!

It was then that Bob threw all of his humiliation and pain into the final desperate last-ditch attempt to wrench us out of our predicament. The action that Bob performed was to try to convey to the Chief a gesture of goodwill - it was an out of character and very bizarre action and we never spoke of it afterwards - never.

It was as though this was a big choreographer's dance number - a tribute to Bob Fosse!! The body has its limits but my vision of Bob knew no boundaries. He somehow had himself centered, under control, and his talent just flourished. Having cleared his throat Bob eloquently began to entertain us with an amazing lively jig type dance with kind of leaping and almost athletic moves. In fact the moves were more reminiscent of an entertaining and colourful aerobics class than the art of traditional dance.

I thought maybe I was hallucinating, I saw a side to Bob that I never realized existed. He was dynamic and had definite star quality! Well Bob held the 'stage' for around ten exhaustive minutes and with sweat in his eyes he finally took his bow.

Bob pulled a pack of cigarettes from his shirt pocket, shook one halfway out, and offered it to the Chief. For the second time that evening I looked in disbelief as the Chief accepted the cigarette. Bob shook out another one, put it between his lips, and flicked a gold Zippo into flame, holding it toward the Chief whilst they both kept their eyes on one another. Bob then closed the lid on the Zippo and handed to the Chief as a token of his appreciation.

God held my mind for awhile that miraculous evening and I think that because of it I tend to love my fellow man a little more today - or at least perhaps I go more gently on him. One thing was for sure, from that point onwards, Bob's rifle was no longer any significant point of reference - the 'Lucky's' were though!

The Chief took the Zippo from Bob and began to clap his hands slowly in a sort of mock applause. He glinted at us both unemotionally and yet given the circumstances, any type of positive acknowledgment was gratefully received.

From that moment on, I knew that we were back on track and that the remainder of the evening would just follow a normal course.

Even today I try not to think about what might have easily occurred.

Later on when we were back across the border, Bob remarked that even the Lord must have been surprised at the outcome that day. He said "I guess the Lord was able to empathize some with us. The predicament that all of us petty mortals found ourselves in, was not so new to the Lord; inasmuch that Adam was always pretty messed-up (but Eve was relatively OK) and that Cain and Abel were a mishmash of discord to the Lord right from the get-go in any event!"

There are some kinds of crooked looks and crow's feet that no amount of modern make-up can hide. Just as there are some kinds of murderous intentions that are blatantly clear from the onset.

Now I'm not at odds with the Chief's resolve, but why did he allow Bob and me to just walk away with the kid. Inasmuch that I would have presumed that the very least we deserved was a good drubbing. Several days after the fragile rumpus I spoke to Mom regarding my deliberations and this is pretty much the way she explained it all to me:

"It's so sad, civilization as it flows past their doors, seems to have entrapped the Indians in it's back-wash. It's absorbing them more and more into the aggressive ways of the white race. Without any animosity they have nevertheless seen through us - we have given them plenty of good reasons. There have been occasions in the past where even a so-called friendly hand from the government turned out to have a knife concealed in it; so yes, they were *reckoning on a visit from you and Bob*

The justification behind why the child was so conversely permissioned-off to reside with Bob lies in the fact that despite Bob's felonious transgressions, he is nonetheless the kid's inherent and natural protector

Straight lines are sometimes difficult responsibilities to walk - sometimes they are good for little more than proving that we're sober on the highway! Be that as it may, in an Indian society were reverence is still held into account, it is often a prerequisite for young men to schooled in fatherhood - there are very few 'absentee' first Americans. And so it would serve little purpose for the child to weep as an orphan - and I guess the mother's somewhat immature nature was also taken into account"

Perhaps the Indian council had permitted a kind of loosening of judgment in Bob's case - him being a minister of the Church and such - but I think now that he has gone from 'local', he should stay gone, or the next time he might be gone!"

It seems to me that Mom's evaluations were right on the button!

Why is it that both Americans and Europeans like to have the last word? It's as though even in the event that they receive a real beating they somehow feel they have won by having the last word.

In Bob's case it was his universal gesture, the phallic finger! Tis as well that the Iroquoian meaning of such differs from ours!!

After Bob and me left Onondaga and in spite of the good outcome, Bob kept bitching on and on about "all the gnat and mosquito bites on the kid". He kept repeatedly splashing the youngster with his eau-de-cologne. The kid's eyes just glinted at Bob in such an unemotional way - I assume that may have been the 'Indian' in him!

I guess the whole caboodle of events that went down at Onondaga was a mighty useful Iroquoian learning experience for both Bob and me.

Sometimes the nights still make me nervous; not for any good reason except from time to time they catch me with my guard down and thinking too deeply over Onondaga.

I shouldn't really be afraid of the darkness and I'm not, however, sometimes the nights still make me nervous.

Let the morning be...

...You must treat the days respectfully, you must be a day yourself, and not interrogate it like a college professor. The world is enigmatical - everything said, and everything known or done - and must not be taken literally, but genially. We must be at the top of our condition to understand anything rightly. You must hear the birds song without attempting to render it into nouns and verbs Cannot we be a little abstemious and obedient? Cannot we let the morning be?

Ralph Waldo Emerson

CHAPTER FOURTEEN

Into segments

In 1940 Jean Christian Sibelius the Finnish composer abruptly ceased composing and spent the rest of his life as a recluse. Before he died during 1957 he destroyed an abundance of his music - perhaps the core component of his life's work. I often wonder, when I hear his work whether or not there are pieces of that core component missing. Are there just too many blanks, too many intermissions? Is there an imbalance that only he can detect - that deep cavity hole that only the composer can see? It seems to me that there is a core component planted in all of us; it is irrepressible, irreplaceable and irremediable once it is lost, and the whole notion of event diminished.

It is uncanningly queer how life has this unexpected habit of making what seemingly is the foreseeable future never actually happen and yet it is the unforeseeable that become a core component of your life.

It's over

Goodbye! She knew of no other way to say it. Leroy Strooduhs was dead, imperceptibly (apparently!) swept away whilst listening to Brahms on his old phonograph. And what of Kim? Arms and head seemingly disengaging, smile unsmiling and almost always receding, voice faded and not really there. So too the faces she saw on the people gathered to listen to her; unforgiving, austere and aloof as if by some sort of cruel conspiracy that had been prearranged - least-ways that's the way it figured to Kim.

The dove was still perched haplessly upon the illusionist's well worn shoulder as he hastened toward the exit to some rather catchy catcalls - however, the rancoured audience sat transfixed when a gawky thirteen year old (going on thirty!) in a frilly costume and funny Dutch bob, tilted her snub nose at them and tapped danced her rhythmical heart out to "swing time". No doubt she'll be invited back again!

Bettina Coogan was the matriarchal head of the Wilkinson Agency on King Street and had chosen Mandy Cohns Club for Kim. "It's unpretentious yet glamorous; homey yet exciting - a good all-round establishment" she said.

Now 'all-round' or not, I was in Kim's dressing room when she came off stage that night. She took me aside, looked at me stony-faced; took a beat and said "everything is over, I can't do it again". I stared into her face, it was as though somebody had turned out the lights in her eyes.

Whatever Kim's relationship was with Jacques, it was finished, but my friendship with Kim was not. We had managed to survive, and remain good friends, in part because I knew she still held Jacques dear to her. When she was with Jacques I never had the feeling that I had to like her because of Jacques; I liked Kim for herself and for the way she would make Jacques 'bloom' when she <u>was</u> with him.

Back to that evening at Mandy Cohns: it always seemed to me that singing in certain downtown clubs and bars was an art that cannot automatically be taught. It can however, be learned, but it requires an awful lot of patience, tolerance and most of all, emotional faith in yourself. The noxious nature of some of those 'elite' establishments downtown requires in essence an impervious thick-skinned approach to their complexities. Though I knew how much Kim needed some tutelage in worldliness, given my own immaturity I could not provide it. I was not capable of being enough of a friend that I truly wanted to be. I guess in our own ways we both lacked an understanding the major deeper themes of life. How could I ever had explained to Kim in those days, that to be a competent high-flyer on stage also requires you to be capable of having a masochistic love affair as and when required! Perhaps on second thoughts Kim possessed that unrecognizable tendency all along - but we both were incapable of seriously spotting it!

The loss of voice

Sometimes I'm sorry for myself for having known her; but then again if I hadn't of known her and I hadn't of memorized her voice so prodigiously, there wouldn't be any valid reason for me to write so untiringly about her, to you all!

The news about Kim reached me as I lay in bed that evening listening to Madame Butterfly on the radio and ostentatiously drawing comparables between Maria and Kim. "Sweet potato to a yam" I encapsulated, as CHML cut in with a news flash:-

 - they implied that her career may be over, after another sudden nightclub   departure!

It's staggering how Kim never became fully conscious of the fact that she was constantly being scrutinized, reported on, and sometimes lied about by the media. Ignorance, said someone who wasn't, is bliss - and Kim was such a blissful person! Jacques had always kept certain realities away from her and now that he was gone they were hitting her head-on and openly.

I turned the radio off and lay there pensively brooding. Only the hands on the clock moved and even they seemed to have no destination any longer.

The clock - even by its very own definition, round and timeless - an expression of deepest, darkest infinity. Was this it for Kim? Had all that she achieved just become simply a throw-away cast down representation of her life?

Tick, Tock!   It's strange how it takes sound to define silence:
                like the clock in the library or the fly in the
                waiting room - they are all topologically interrelated.

Tick, Tock!   It's strange how even the infinite can adjust itself to
                our needs: Like the deaf audience of seven who hear
                so miraculous when your phrasing has lost control of
                itself.

Tick, Tock!   It's strange how fidgeting and imprecation can be
                disregarded just by staring at the back of the
                room as through the sun shone there.

Tick, Tock!   It's strange how they leave you alone at two to crawl
                by yourself and fall by yourself. And it's strange that

without much attention - from two onwards – it's the same story. Only the sense of distance changes.

Kim's free-fall was frightening - a spinning, weaving, toppling legend just waiting for the impact: voice knotted, body withering. The electricity of being this amazing human battery, charged by the reckless appreciation of others had become seriously all chewed up!

CHAPTER FIFTEEN

'belle dame sans merci personified'

Around Christmas mistletoe has its own unique kissing role to play. Whereas, numerous seemingly Christian acts at Christmas are in actuality Pagan in origin, it seems to be that mistletoe/kissing is (whichever way you choose to construe it) truly Christian. Withal it symbolises the love of Christ for all mankind. In any event if only as a licence for intimacy it has retained a great popularity and perhaps become a little more sexual and a little less than sacred as the years have passed by.

Eight months is definitely too long to have to wait for someone to get healthy, especially when their sanity is in question and you are hurtfully angry. And so by and by Sarah Smith stopped coming to visit her mother at the Brentville Institution.

Like many a bright lingerer of daydreams she was positive that in the city she would be able to seek out all of the explanations and the configurations that had repeatedly side-stepped her kitty-cornered life. And so that's where she scooted; headlong!

It wasn't long after that she emerged on the standpoint outside of Arless Shoes opposite Gore Park. Selling sprigs of mistletoe and giving out kisses and peddling the books of matches she had swiped from 'Chicken Roost' next door. From daybreak 'till dawn she was doing powerfully well. She had a sort of avant-garde cuteness and folks are more Indian/charity inclined around Christmas in any event. She was just getting ready to hunker down for the night when a juiced-up moron came out of Duffy's and swiped her across the head with a bottle of social values! I always had a mental image of that SOB as being probably Five-Four in elevator shoes! And then again I visualise my hero 'Shane' and loathe myself for being disparaging over small people. Sarah, in fact, didn't even catch a glimpse of him, she went out like a light does.

Kim was on her way home from some downtown dirt club when she came across Sarah nightmaring in Arless Store's doorway.

The moon was lighting up her little pink shoes protruding out of the doorway into the gray snow. There were many passers and many more wide-eyed, wide-birth thoughtful characters who avoided her like she may pass-on some serious syphilitic disease or such. When it's Christmas shopping time and all of the parking lots are full, the streets of any city can be a profound and muddy locale to drown in. And who really cares about the bothersome final breaths of an Indian itinerant anyways - the graveyards stay open for their mournful serviceability right through Xmas day. It's only the all important 'Shop 'n Save' store or the 'going-out-of-business' sale whom the populous support. Christmas can be a very one-dimensional occasion.

Having said that it was Kim who gave all her womanly smiles away to a passing cab driver who gratefully flew by his shirt-tails to the 'Lady of Mercy' charity infirmary on Dundas & Vine.

In no time there was an ecclesiastical assembly line of Sisters earnestly attending to Sarah's woes: stitches and needlework extemporized to perfection - dabs of Friar's Balsam skilfully preventing the bleeding - antiseptic Permanganate of Potash poured into a tepid bath - dressing gowned and tucked away between pristine bed linen (+ a tranquillizer or two!). It really was a determined and noble accomplishment by the Sisters and Kim (being Kim) compensated them very generously afterwards.

Kim sat silently by Sarah's bedside, the tranquillizers had done their job and Sarah was really beginning to 'send the cows home'. Kim gazed at Sarah steadily and intently, she was becoming kind of consumed by Sarah's unfactitious and cardinal beauty: her hair was straight, dark and almost endlessly long and had become tangled yet still fell into place of its own accord in a softly beautiful fashion. Her eyes were slightly slanted and she had an over well-shaped mouth with startling white teeth. Kim guessed that she was around thirteen years of age, yet without a discernible curve or breast in site. Her skin was kind of honey-tan shade which looked as if it had been acquired under the sun. On the other hand Kim's faded white sallowness emphasized it all quite a bit and made Kim feel vaguely uncomfortable and overly curious about herself and her maternal inclinations - if that is what they were?

Hamilton Ontario – circa 1962
Spot: Duffys, Arless and Chicken Roost to the far right of the photo!

CHAPTER SIXTEEN

Simplify, Simplify (Thoreau)

By and by Kim's values were becoming partly inconsistent and conflictingly uncomfortable at the very least. Her voice, once a virtue, had become a vexatious liability to her. She felt a need or desire to have or to do something else. She craved to feel released and liberated and at a distance from the burdensome and gruelling worry that her assetted voice demanded.

A scissor wind was cutting through the backyard eaves; maple leafs lie frozen on the pond. A light snow falls and begins to connect riverbank to riverbank. The eternal magic of eternal things that sends the ingenuous out into the world and brings them home again had arrived.

Sarah had settled on Kim's couch beside the fire - warm, comfortable like a single summers day. Coffee cup balancing on her lap, this was Sarah's invulnerable yet peculiarly imperious haven. In the past it had never been warm enough for Kim yet lately she felt that some kind of 'transmogrification' was so queerishly circulating through all parts of her body toward her heart.

Sarah was learning to drink tea and how to say 'yes' instead of 'yeah' The knife is on the right side of the setting where she supposed the fork should be; and they should be placed together when the meal is finished - not, spread-eagled!

Kim had become the matriarchal parent and Sarah was deemed Kim's adultish child, the chattel of Kim's repressed creativity. Kim was the nurturer in a screwball sense to her expectations, and it wasn't going to work!

The constant fears that Kim haggled with over Sarah were never going to be eradicated by unrealistic expectations. It was almost as though Kim needed her beliefs for the future in order to give herself back the identity she had lost in the past. The alchemy of balance tired and emotional; Kim's over-stretched, upside down search for self-enlightenment was never going to be a solution for her hunger. It was as though Kim had an expectation of catastrophe and a need in her to 'be' tormented! I was always fearful that this extremity of emotion would either destroy her or improve her life, but it would never become just a learning process for her.

CHAPTER SEVENTEEN

Wistfulness

It was going to be a Charles Ives winter. Even this early on you could tell by the way the branches trembled after dark and the wind raked up the leaves. The freckled night was moving into day now, Kim sat half dressed at her bedroom window, eyes wide open, looking fixedly at the blank windows in the building across the street - her expression was as empty as theirs.

It seemed to Kim that Sarah and her had come so close during the past several months and yet she oftentimes was fearful that Sarah might imagine that it was too long. It was the way in which Sarah had a habit of treating her advice like it was unworthy of serious consideration. When Kim was growing up she needed somebody and right now she needed Sarah to stay, a while longer: at least until the baby was born. Sarah had quickly gotten all fired-up when Kim suggested that her 'longings' for various foods were unnatural! Said that she had known cases where a mother had a child born with unusual birthmarks, because she had given into her 'longings' Said that mother and child share the same blood and she should choose her diet with great care. She should forget these strange cravings and that strength of will and common sense will do it for her if she has the inclination.

CHAPTER EIGHTEEN

'Robert'

A morning song that can shiver
quiet backwaters
of the future and fill
their waves and silt with hope

Federico Garcia Lorca

Sarah remembered hearing children in the street outside, she remembered the noise of pots & pans in the kitchen and Kim and the midwife bickering - all above her own noise. This was her bed, her room. Her world; how she envied them all for the day long sunshine. Kim played everything from Bach to The Supremes to help lower the pain but ultimately it became chloroform's reinforcement that put Sarah to sleep.

Perhaps after all 16 years of age is old enough to dig a well, sow several kids and even curse if you so desire, in any event it was Sarah's last day as a child. The silent rain was falling and lovers still sat in the park unscathed under their Mother Theresa umbrellas, oblivious as perhaps they should be to the sad mistaken heart and the loneliness of childbirth.

Sarah's baby was a boy - for Sarah and her baby it was all worth it. It seems to me that the price you pay for sunshine can sometimes be quite dear when all you have to sell is youth. However, when you are Indian poor you only have yourself but at least all of you is yours.

Kim gave the baby to her, the midwife had tied a diaper around his tiny head - Kim said he looked an awful lot like a Polish peasant. He had what looked like a cat's claw mark upon his cheek and another on his ankle - the midwife said that first born's are often marked but that the marks would be gone in a few days. The marks endured and everso the child - Sarah named him Robert, said it was a 'Godly' name. Practicing or otherwise 'Bob' with all his faults was indeed devoutly spiritual!

CHAPTER NINETEEN

Departure

This morning I woke up just in time to see
a yellow Unicorn
Eating the low branches from the linden tree outside -
Then into the green he ran
and was gone.

Rod McKuen

The freckled day was moving into night now. The house was quieter than usual, it had that kind of museum sound about it, the sort of sound that can only come from you. Kim moved silently and aimlessly from room to room as though trying to disentangle herself from the patterns of hysterical unrest that were pervading her mind. All in all it was a curiously disturbing evening, imbued with a sense of purpose that was old and withered, used up, and done... And inasmuch that Sarah and Robert were expected to be home hours ago!

So often Kim had stood in that public mirror of inequity and watched her infancy and early childhood being played out before her tired eyes. So often she would ask questions..."let's not talk about it now" - that's what Mama would say!

Kim told me that Mama used to smile a lot but never once to anyone who she didn't care about. And when Mama frowned you had to question her repeatedly to find out the reason why - although you seldom ever did.

Nowhere in any of Kim's mother's personal effects were there anything about Kim's father. Absolutely nothing. Not that I thought there would be.

Cogitating on so many foolish things, Kim finally wandered through to Sarah's bedroom in order to turn the bed down - a humble domestic ritual that her 'Mama' had taught her. She paused and frowned questionably at a note safety pinned to Sarah's pillow, it emphatically explained:

"Now that the winter has come and gone I'll say good-bye. I am fully recovered and so you must please lose all trace of me - living my life indefinitely by a stranger's hand is not our way"
The note was unfussily signed "Sarah".

Perhaps Kim had tried too hard to set up Sarah's future in the ashes and the dust of her own woeful past. It was distinctly a cruelty of sorts, however, the question inextricably is; for who and from whence? It seems to me that some things you can borrow but never own - after a while it's time to say good-bye to everything.

CHAPTER ONE of Book One, elucidated

When all at once your fractured heart has stopped beating and turned to gypsum. When so unexpectedly all of the most important details that used to stimulate your thought turn to brick-coloured pieces of shrapnel. And when there are no longer any nuances to your facial expression except for deadpan and it takes pills and coffee to uplift your drowning articulation - then perhaps now is the best time to throw away that sketch of the great utopia; it is frayed and it has been trampled over too many times!

Kim had so inadvertently gone way past the extreme limit of her piecemeal resources. All of the eagerness and the pig-headed and wilful expectations of her astounding optimism had vanished - passed away into total oblivion. What made her tick had come to the end of its tether, her umbilical link to lucidity had severed itself and her world was now proceeding menacingly inward.

As all the Heavens were a bell,
And being, but an Ear,
And I, and silence, some strange race
Wrecked, solitary here -

Emily Dickinson

The sky was uncaring, motionless and heavy with snow. It was indubitably the worst winter since '52. Hamilton got hammered on Monday be a savage lake-effect snowstorm that dumped 36 inches in 7 hours shutting down streets, offices and the International airport.

"So, we had a good Fall and a great summer anyways, ya know? Whaddy a gonna do?" said Giuseppe Esposito, working his takeout counter at his pizza parlour on King Street E.

The sombre afternoon shadows were creeping lazily across the motel drapes, Kim sat on the edge of her bed stock-still and silent, boxed in by whiteness, overtaken by gray she just desired to know what words of sensibility were left for her, if any. Of all those doors of delight she had helped to open, they all seemed to have slammed shut when momentarily she had looked the other way.

Had Kim come to this? Unable and unsure how to fill up even one more day alone.

A whimper succeeded by a shiver and followed by a shambolic shrug and gathering her last trace of pertinacity she all at once realized that whether it be punishment or retribution the infinite time for resolve had surfaced for her.

Kim bundled her more treasured belongings in a Passé Tower's travel bag; the remaining items of clothing etc., - those with too many memories, she just put them out with the trash. It could be that the full significance of Kim's decision was yet to be determined, withal it was not a remarkable decision to make under the circumstances; however, moment to moment it was in fact a gigantic decision of sorts.

The snow boomed from the North-East like a drawn-out organ note as Kim tottered slipping and sliding across Maple Street toward the bus station on Brant. What of her decision, if the bus was not running today?; a sudden uncontrollable fear struck her - in the loneliness of winter, imagination can easily overtake your reality.

The bus was warm and welcoming. Kim believed that the driver had given her a 'knowing' smile. In any event he reminded her of a college boy she had once dated, and that made her smile back at him.

As the bus began its journey to anywhere Kim gazed dreamily through the tinted glass windows and out into the neon lit night. She breathed her cigarette smoke in deeply and marvelled at the scuttles full of powdered Ontario snow falling from the heavens. It made her recall Jacques telling her "envelop me as I envelop you" and now it only applied to the snow!

She loved this Greyhound stealthily taking her away from those dour yesterday memories; across the hills and down to somewhere she had never been.

Kim watched the cedars and jagged firs flickering by and making distance almost a certainty, when sleep came and compassionately devoured her...

I find any sleep
that claims to be
a sleep of reason
unreasonable and fitful
yet each night
I fall down in darkness
all the same
wondering what new land
knows the sound
of singing swallows

Rod McKuen (Fields of Wonder)

~ end ~

Limberlost forecourt

ADDENDUM

After trying to put some sort of reverent distance – which is what I thought I needed – between myself and the finalised chapters of Limberlost III, I incurably found my mind pondering over a query that my proof-reader had inadvertently mentioned when we were working on Chapter 18.
To wit; she was curious over "What became of Sarah Smith?"

From a proof-read perspective Kaye Brzozka is an exceptional person of astute disposition. However, whether we always agree upon my heterogeneous punctuation and grammar is almost certainly open to question! Though it does seem to me that Kaye was right to the button regarding the Sarah Smith issue; and that being the case I will respond to her question – otherwise 'snap beans' will be crawling through my psyche forevermore!

On a clear bright winter morning of Monday December 29th 1890, a detachment of the 7th Cavalry (Custer's regiment) stood guard over several hundred refugee Sioux. Yellow Bird, a Sioux shaman, stood up, gazed into the distance and threw a handful of dirt into the air. The cavalry, who were in all likelihood pretty much psyched up, mistakenly assumed it to be a signal for the Sioux to attack and consequently they opened fire, killing and wounding dozens upon dozens of innocent Sioux. Such, in essence, is the 'battle of Wounded Knee'.

During 1973, activists from the American Indian Movement staged an armed protest at Wounded Knee – they called it Wounded Knee II. That was where my trail to Sarah Smith led me. Apparently she was part of a ragtag film crew who were subsequently arrested and charged with "aiding a civil disorder". Two Indians were killed during the 70 day skirmish with some 150 officers injured.

The judge was a dark good-looking man called Quanah Hooper. Transcripts say that he was two thirds Indian himself. In any event perhaps that was why he felt suitably sympathetic to Sarah and her mangy compatriots. Although they all got away with just a rigorous reprimand and were allowed to leave the court, I guess it all worked out abstemiously for the town's coffers as well. Inasmuch that by the time they had reached the towns limits, Sarah had given birth in an irrigation ditch to another son. According to my check-mark regarding Sarah's children, that was child number five (kindly be it so!). Unpositively Sarah was likely as not 26 years of age.

Sarah and her children had an adequate abode in 'Tent City' just north east of Alamo Junction on the edge of the town. It was a friendly little community, everybody knew everybody else. Some of the tents such as Sarah's were more of a permanent nature and they had board floors which were easy to scrub down and keep clean. The tents were lit by kerosene lamps and they all looked kind of beguiling at night-time. Nonetheless they were pretty flimsy when the wind got up, and one such night sparks from a coal-oil stove ignited Sarah's tent and spread to several others. Despite the valiant efforts of bucket brigades there was no putting the fires out; their meagre possessions were gone in moments. Like cats they clawed through the scattered debris the next day, it was a necessary thing to do, but pointless.

I know that they slept rough in a public park for several nights but after, they moved along and disappeared behind all those yonder trees; I lost track of them again.

It seems that afterwards there was a whole gap in the Smiths' lives that was unaccounted for.

Although from time to time I would really intensify my investigations and at one stage I even hired an agency who came up with zilch. I started to view both old mail and new mail with more care – now, no matter how remote a possibly seemed I tried to follow it up.

I decided to visit Bob at the Limberlost one 'dark' evening to get his viewpoint on where Sarah and her kids had disappeared to. It wasn't a very well thought out idea – visiting Bob that is. He gave me a kind of sermonised homily – the gospel according to Bob! I guess it was what I should have expected; if memory serves it went something like this: "Which is the better woman – she who doeth twice as much as she is asked or she that doeth just as much as she is asked?" He paused and looked me straight in the eye. Just when I assumed that he wasn't going to continue, he did! "She that doeth twice as much as she is asked, she is the better woman and she will be redeemed for all of her spunky efforts!"

I guess that during Sarah's adolescents (and my own too, for that matter) in those droll closing years of the 1950's and the zigzagging early years of the 1960's, the bomb had left us with a new world that nobody was quite sure about. Morals, political philosophy and religion were all very much in a state of suspension. Jack, Bobby, Dr King, some of us like to think that we recovered; perhaps Sarah Smith just never did?

However, that wicked wolf of cumulative chaos never did get to devour Little Red Sarah Smith in her entirety because behind yonder trees a trail of kids had led me undauntedly to the renowned cottage of a brave wood chopper from New Bruswick (in point of fact he worked for the Forestry Commission!) and unremarkably he was so greatly enamoured by her beauty and whisked her off to safety forthwith!

The closing mention that I have of Sarah is as a somewhat young grandma (too shy to come to the telephone and speak to me). By all accounts she loves her French toast with wild mountain blackberry syrup – boiled carrots, wieners and beans and fried egg sandwiches. So says Zee (as well) waitress at 'Kellys Diner'.

As during Sarah's fertility days, perhaps her dexterity was to flub the chub* successfully and remain handsome; leastways she is living happily ever after at last, and that's all that really matters!

Positively The End!

* Flub the chub – to try and pinch someone where they are fat!

About Ricky Dale

Ricky Dale was born in England and raised in West Africa and North America; his mother referred to the family as being of 'Colonial' nationality.

Ricky's singing career began in 1959 with one-nighters, college dates and the occasional radio show. As fame increased, he began to-ing and fro-ing across the Atlantic between the UK and Canada, charming capacity audiences in clubs and theatres. An individual style and heartfelt rendering of ballads and the contrast of his wild Rock 'n Roll were, he says "inspired from the hope and energy of West Africa". As the 60's developed Ricky began to shun the glare of celebrity. Studios, clubs and stages pulsed with drugs and a tragic mass entertainment of messed-up so-called music was becoming mainstream. After a long absence from the stage, he completed contractual obligations in Niagara, Canada and Southampton, England and faded into obscurity.

In 2000 Ricky, with his daughter Kim, visited Canada. "It was a kind of odyssey to the past", he says. Their poignant journey encompassed the Brant Inn location in Burlington, Ontario. Decades before, as an enterprising teenager from England, he stepped into the limelight of this fabulous nightclub and truly perfected his craft.
In that golden era a host of glamorous stars entertained the Brant's sophisticated audiences. Ricky had fronted the Guy Lombardo Band, duetted with the sheer genius Danny Kaye and had been 'mothered' by the beautiful Jayne Mansfield: "When the old-timers were mean to me, she provided sympathetic company where I could escape at will and complain. The Brant Inn was tragically torn down in around 1970, but as Kim and I stood on the shore of Lake Ontario (near Maple Avenue), we could easily imagine the melodies that had floated out across the lake: sometimes reality is not permitted to be an intruder!"

Ricky was MD of several innovative companies in the West of England for 21 years and now spends his time writing.

Final farewell at Anville Railway Station

"Le temps que I'on prend pour dire: Je taime, c'est le seul qui reste au bout de nos jours"